hunting by the river

Black Shuck Books
www.blackshuckbooks.co.uk

First published in Great Britain in 2024 by
Black Shuck Books
Kent, UK

Versions of the following stories have previously appeared in print:
'Roots' in *Black Static #75* (2020)
'Hunting by the River' in *Black Static #69* (2019)
'Flotsam' in *Tales from the Shadow Booth Volume 1* (2017)
'Habitual' in *For Tomorrow* (Black Shuck Books, 2024)
'All the Honours That Are Due' in *The Lonely Crowd #10* (2018)
'A Visitor's Guide to Penge Magic (Annotated)' in *BFS Horizons #8* (2019)
'They Have Gone to the City' in *Cloisterfox #1* (2022)
'Stabbed in the Neck by Dot Cotton' online at unsungstories.co.uk (2015)
'A Moment Could Last Them Forever' in *Unthology 10* (Unthank Books, 2016)

Set in Caslon
Cover art and interior design © WHITEspace, 2024
www.white-space.uk

978-1-913038-88-5

Hunting by the River

by

Daniel Carpenter

BLACK
SHUCK
BOOKS

Hunting by
the River

by

Daniel Carpenter

BLACK
SHUCK
BOOKS

For Nici, Sadie and Robin

| Contents |

~

Contents

'I dreamed I saw you dead in a place by the water. A ravaged place. All flat and empty and wide open. And you were covered in some kind of binding. Like a mummy. Something white and reflective, from head to toe. And the light shone on you. Oh, how it shone on you! It glanced off you, and it was like a pure, bright silver. The wind was singing. It sang: you have suffered enough. You have suffered enough. Then death came and he kissed you. Lightly. Gently. Upon the lips. There is nothing beyond, he whispered, only me, only me. There is nothing beyond. Only me.'

Nicola Barker, *Wide Open*

'A city is not a natural occurrence.'

Rowland Atkinson, *Alpha City*

|Roots|

Dennis was the one who struck it, but he'd quickly backed away, realising that what he was looking at was a small hand. It seemed to him, at first anyway, to belong to a mannequin, though it only took a few moments for him to know with certainty that it wasn't. Human. Pale. A child's. He'd dropped the spade and scrambled back. Others on the site with him came over. Was everything alright? What had got his knickers in a twist? Bloody newbie can't take it in the heat. But then they all saw what he'd seen. Someone called the foreman over, bruiser of a man called Churchill. The lingering scent of cigars that followed him wafted in and Dennis felt sickness rising.

'Come on lad,' Churchill said, hauling him to his feet, 'cuppa in the office.'

To one of the others, he said, 'Phone. Now.'

The tea didn't help. He saw the lights of the police car approach, bouncing off the walls. The distant open/shut of the doors and the crunch of boots on the site floor. Churchill was out there with them. Dennis was alone in the office. He sent a text to Mary, explaining what had happened. A body, he described it as. Though that wasn't strictly true. He'd found a hand. That was all. Young though.

In the small firms with the old timers, he'd heard stories about finding bodies. *Not so rare in London* they'd said. *Bet you got none of that in that arse end of nowhere where you come from.* It was true. One of them, Phil, had been part of a team that had found a plague pit whilst on the Crossrail job.

'Thirty bodies they found,' he'd said. One of the young lads, kid called Petey, thought it was contagious and fucked off to A&E. That was how it was. The old had seen it all. The young were stupid. Dennis was old, but new. He didn't exist in the stories.

Churchill came into the office.

'We've had to shut down, maybe for a little while.' He sat down, took off his hard hat and rubbed his bald head. 'Tea alright? Think the rest of the lads are off down the pub. Be good for you to go along with them.'

'How many bodies?' Dennis asked.

'It's a police matter now. If you like, I can refer you to another firm. I know a guy up in Stratford working on a new development there.'

Outside, Dennis saw more lights blinking. Others were coming.

None of them talked about it in the pub. Someone bought Dennis a lager and he sat nursing it for a while, pretending to drink. They talked football and Dennis slipped into it easily, letting it wash over him, forgetting things. The booze did that too, after a while, and he found himself into his third pint, the sun long set. Outside, a drizzle had set in and he thought about home, the countryside showers, the smell of petrichor and manure. The cold of stone tiles. He needed a piss.

In the toilets, one of the Polish kids from the site – Aleksy, Dennis thought his name was – stood at the urinal. He caught Dennis' eye.

'It was you, no?'

'Me?'

'Who found them. Was you, wasn't it?'

He nodded, though it took him a moment to even register what the lad was on about. He couldn't have been more than eighteen, nineteen. Skinny frame, alabaster skin. Not like the beer guts and sunburned tan of the others.

'How far down did they go?'

It didn't make sense to him, but then he was a few pints in, so he just murmured a non-answer and finished up. Aleksy followed him to the sink.

'Who was growing them? That's what I want to know.'

The Stratford job was further for him, but easy work. Perhaps they were worried about his age, or his lack of experience. Perhaps the story of the hand had made its way across the city, site to site. Either way, it felt as though they were taking pity on him. The pay was fine though, so he didn't complain. He was sweeping up debris from one of the floors in the building and he looked out at the east of the city. The remains of the Olympics, that red tower rising so close to him, and beyond it, the River Lea and the tiny Wick Woodland. Things grew there the way the buildings went up. If you looked away just for a while, you wouldn't notice and then, suddenly something new would be complete and there. Bushes and leaves and flats and tiny homes blocking your view. It was Stratford this month and he'd already heard of a job coming up in Peckham.

They ended up in a pub near the site, crowded with after work drinkers. There were ten of them and they fought their way to a table. Dennis noticed Aleksy mingling amongst them. He hadn't even known that the lad was on site with him. One of the others got a round in, and Aleksy brought the hand up.
      'Dennis found it. Over in Battersea, at the Power Station.'
      They all talked. They all had stories.
      'Still shut down, has been for weeks.'
      'Go by on the train sometimes. There's a white tent, size of a bloody wedding marquee. People in hazmat suits going in.'
      'Hundreds of them. Maybe thousands. Reaching up.'
      Dennis listened, he had nothing to add. He'd only started the story, set up the foundations. The others, they had more experience, they knew how to build it up and grow it.
      The stories became wilder, more unbelievable. One of them said they'd discovered eyeballs on stalks, watching from under the dirt in Catford. Another told of how only a year ago, a bush of yellowing, tobacco-stained teeth was cut down unceremoniously in the middle of The City.
      'I never saw anything about the bodies in the news,' Dennis said.
      Aleksy and the others laughed. Someone slapped him on the back. *You don't get it* the slap said. *You don't get it at all.*

Walking back to the station with Aleksy they stopped in a kebab shop and hazily ordered some food. The two of them sat on plastic seats and tried to pretend that the bright lights weren't bothering them.
      'We could go see them,' Aleksy said. 'I want to see them.'

'They won't be there still,' Dennis replied, looking down at his can of ginger beer. 'They'll be at the morgue, or somewhere, I don't know. People don't just leave corpses in a hole for months. That's not how it works.'

But he could see the determination in Aleksy's eyes. A youthful spark of something. A daring that he didn't have any longer. They parted ways at Canada Water, Dennis tired, Aleksy twitching with nervous excitement.

On the way south, sitting on the Overground he passed rows of terraced houses. Old homes that had stood there for decades, some nearly a century. Places with their roots in the city. Every now and then, the land opened up and something new stood in the middle. The framework for a block of flats. The glass edifice of an office, wasteland surrounding it. Those new buildings, he thought, looked lonely. Exposed. He thought about leaving the city. Going back up north. Not that that would be any better. The cities, everywhere, were expanding, growing out, fighting for space in a metropolitan forest.

They re-opened the Battersea site. Whatever had been dug up was long gone. The white marquee that someone mentioned had vanished. Where Dennis had struck the hand there was now a ditch, a few metres deep. Aleksy hadn't come back to the site, probably working on another job somewhere else. There was no shortage of work in London.

He was with five others, pouring concrete into the foundations, when Churchill approached. Dennis could see the cigar peeking out of his pocket, his yellowing teeth in a visible grin.

'All good over here?'

The others with Dennis nodded. Churchill slapped him on the back.

'Heard good things about you. People talk you know. Think we might be able to get you onto something a bit challenging, if you're man enough.'

It wouldn't be much, not yet, but it was a step up. A chance to really get his hands dirty. Dennis imagined himself a gardener. Dreamt about it that night, watching himself working, as though he was Aleksy or Churchill. He was standing over a patch of dirt. They were standing over a patch of dirt. You were standing over a patch of dirt, bending down, pulling out weeds shaped like rebar and insulation, planting pipes and steel bars. But there were people too, and you watered plants upon which hundreds of small seedling babies screamed and wailed and cried, and you found the ones that you'd raised, the children, and harvested them, ready to plant elsewhere, ready to let them grow new roots, new cities.

|What They Say About Cat Killers|

~

They found the cat in the rain, out by the back of the bike racks. Blood splattered all up the walls next to where Mo tagged *King of This* again, after the council had washed it off. She'd been the one to find it, when she'd ducked beneath the underpass to escape the storm. All of her lot were still there when I walked under, heading back to the block.

'Ty,' because I'm Michael and tried to box Shaun way back, 'Ty, you want to come see a dead cat?'

'I'm alright Mo,' I tried to walk past them, but she shoved her body in front of me, blocking my way. She was half grinning.

'Someone slashed it up good, blood fuckin' everywhere. Think it was Desmond's, you know: Gizmo.'

Her whole lot were crowded round the thing. I could hear a horrible wet noise as they poked it with a stick.

Gizmo used to walk along the handrails on the tenth floor of the block where Desmond lived. Either he didn't care much about the cat, or he was too senile to see what it was doing every day.

Mo followed me all the way out to the block, and up the stairs. She wouldn't stop going on about it. In the end, I had to say something.

'He probably fell, probably just fell and died.'

'No way man, no way. Proper slashed, I'm telling you. Someone gutted the thing and left it there to die. Just come look.'

I unlocked the front door and tried to get in to the flat as quick as I could but Mo caught the door and held it open. I could tell she was excited about the cat. Nothing got people in the block as excited as blood.

'Have you called the cops?'

'The fuck do you think? Course not. Going to investigate this on our own aren't we? You want in?'

'I'm alright Mo.'

'Fine,' she said, letting go of the doorframe, and closing the gate on me, 'but you know what they say about cat killers.'

I shut the door to the flat, and as she walked away I heard her say, 'Just a matter of time before they move on up.'

I brought my dad his tablets before making myself some dinner. Laid them out on a tray the way I always did, and took them into his room. The blinds were down, and the TV had been on all day. Whatever channel he'd been watching had ended, and the blue holding screen illuminated the room. Dad was asleep, glasses halfway up his forehead. I placed the tray down on the bedside table and leant over, gently lifting the glasses up. I checked the channel. The text on the guide said, 'Channel Off Air'. Probably had been for weeks.

I turned the TV off, and felt the absence of white noise immediately. There was my father's breath, a retching engine-like breathing; the sound of a constant struggle to stay running. He'd wake soon and have his pills then. He always woke himself up.

After eating, a thought came to me. Had anyone told Desmond?

Desmond's flat was way up at the top of the block. Lifts were out, again, so I scrambled up the concrete stairs quick as I could. On the eighth floor, I got a whiff of the weed that Lav sold – proper sharp stuff that overpowered even his mum's cooking. A few floors below, I could hear some couple arguing, the sound echoing up the staircase. Maybe Pete and Vicky, they were always at it.

Up on nine I passed some more of Mo's tags. *King of This*. I stopped for a moment and leant against the railing, pressing my face up against the cracked red bars. Below me, a handful of children played in the courtyard, just metres from where Gizmo had been found. I'd forgotten long ago what children play, but they seemed to be in the middle of a game. Five of them stood in a circle around the sixth, turning clockwise whilst the child in the centre spun in the opposite direction. Their mouths were moving, and they were all whispering to the blindfolded kid, but as far up as I was, I couldn't hear them. They stopped, and the sixth child, blindfolded with his arms outstretched, stepped forwards towards the now mystery child in front of him. When they burst out laughing, it was obvious he'd made a guess, and got it wrong.

Finally I hit the top step on ten. The fluorescent strip lights strung along the concrete roof flickered and my shadow was thrown across the walls in the direction of Desmond's place.

The kids here, they loved it when something bloody happened. Any chance they got to catch a whiff of danger and they were on it. They had heart, but it was like something like this would happen, and that would be it for them. Forget Desmond. Maybe they'd find the cat killer too. Maybe Mo and her lot would teach them a thing or two before the police managed to track them down. After hearing her tell me about what they did to it, a part of me wasn't even fussed about them cutting a bloke like that up. So long as they didn't go too far.

Mo didn't come up here. Not many people did unless they lived here. The lights were broken, and the concrete was as old as it was on any of the other floors, but it was untouched, like an old church. Desmond's place sat at the end of the corridor, and even from where I stood, I could see the telly on in his living room.

I looked down at the courtyard again. The kids were gone. Probably down at the back of the Tesco down the street. That's where they usually went. Asking guys to buy them a beer or two, or trying their luck themselves. Much harder now than I was when I was a kid. Leave them to their games, whatever they may be.

Outside Desmond's flat was his garden: four plant pots packed with whatever would grow all the way up here. I got a good whiff of thyme as I got closer and remembered my dad cooking me food when I'd get back from work. Before he got too ill to do anything. Stuff like that, it's like you suddenly remember just how you felt in that moment. Like a damned time machine in a plant.

Desmond answered the door in his dressing gown, half done up around the waist. His silvery chest hair caught the moonlight and behind it, nearly hidden, I caught a glimpse of the scar that had made him famous around here.

'Michael?' he said, looking over my shoulder like I was part of a trick.

'Something's happened to Gizmo.'

'Oh. You'd better come in then.'

'Who did it?'

I'd grabbed a couple of beers from Desmond's fridge, and we were sat in his front room; the fake warm glow of the strip lighting outside like the window of an oven. The other cats, god knows how many he had, were in every room. Several sprawled on the settee, two stalking above on a raised bookshelf. The silhouette of another could be seen behind the curtain. The whole place stunk of them.

'Don't know. Could be one of the lads from down the road. Could be it was an accident too.'

'Could be them terrorists.'

'Don't think terrorists are going to be going round killing cats.'

He took a swig of beer, his hands shook. 'What about Mo and her lot?'

'What about them?'

'I've seen them about. I know what they do, don't think I don't know Michael. She's got this place under her thumb, and what is she, twelve?'

'She's sixteen, and it doesn't matter. She's got nothing to do with this. Her *lot* are out there right now looking for the,' I paused, because the word felt odd to use in the context of a cat, 'killer.'

'Never did like her. Her father neither. Mum was alright though.'

'You always liked the mums.'

For a while, both of us sat in silence. Not that I found it strange or awkward; the two of us sitting in his living room, with the quiet flicker of the telly on. Silence has always been a natural state for me. Ever since Dad got the way he did I've been able to find comfort in the shared quiet moments we have with one another. It feels like in those moments I understand people a lot more. Desmond finished his beer and tipped it slightly, looking to see if there was any more left in the bottle. Then he looked at me, and I thought he was going to offer me another, but instead he said quietly, 'You know, she was only a kitten, at heart I mean. She still loved to play.'

'I'm sorry.' Then, as an afterthought, 'We'll find who did this.'

'No, you won't.'

I didn't think we would either.

The bird's head was discovered shoved in the end of the drainpipe out near the west block. Lovely little budgie. Dad had taken a turn for the worse and I rode with him all the way in the back of the ambulance as they tried to keep him breathing. The bird had been stuffed right inside the pipe whilst it was still alive. The water on the first three floors stopped working overnight, and in the morning someone saw it bubbling over through the drain. They found the budgie when the plumber took apart the plastic tube to find the blockage. It had been wedged three floors up, and claws had torn scratches into the side.

'Michael,' my dad said between breaths. 'Michael.'

As though he'd just realised who had been with him the whole time.

He got on with all of them in the hospital, not just the nurses either, but the patients too. I stayed as late as I could, till they got him back to normal, and I came back the next day to find him sat bolt upright in the bed, playing shadow puppets with the grandson of the bloke opposite.

'Everything alright Dad?' I asked as the nurse handed me a cuppa.

'Fine, fine. Good as new.' He flexed his thin, limp arm to prove it to me. The boy opposite laughed.

I didn't tell him about the budgie, though it was all anyone was talking about back at the flats. Mo came over one night and I tried to help her with her homework but she wasn't having any of it. Could barely sit still, every few seconds bouncing out of her chair.

'What are they going to go for next?' she said, after the bark of Mrs Latimer's Rottweiler echoed across the courtyard.

I tried to get her back on track, 'Can you tell me what you know about covalent bonds?'

'You know what they say about cat killers?'

I did.

When he was surrounded by people, Dad was the picture of health. When they went, that was when the real him came out. Nurses would pass him pills and he'd smile and laugh and joke, and as soon as they were gone, 'They're poisoning me, you know?'

'Dad, they're not. They're just trying to help.'

All of his hair had gone by then. Almost all the rest of it had gone on that first night in the hospital, as though he'd lain down a bald man, and someone had placed little wispy grey tufts of hair all around him. It was like, the moment he left the block his skin had wrinkled and he'd become an old man, just like that.

Desmond wasn't so cut up about Gizmo anymore. He poured us out some vodka and we leant out over the balcony, looking down. A plane flew low overhead. Every year it felt like they got a little closer to us, or maybe we got a little closer to them.

'How's he doing?'

I thought about my father, lying to everyone in that hospital. I thought about him whispering to me. *They're poisoning me.*

'He'll be fine.' I knocked back the shot.

'This place, it's changing, isn't it?'

There was music playing, somewhere distant. Mo and her lot were out in the park; I'd seen them set off a while ago, three or four on fixie bikes, couple of skateboards, and Mo on foot leading the way. I remembered when they used to play in the courtyard below us.

'Maybe it's not this place. Maybe it's us.'

Desmond sipped his vodka. 'It doesn't feel like that. Everyone changes, Michael, but not like this. It feels like this whole place is infected, like someone buried something here and its roots were rotten and dead, and it's coming up, and it's growing. Soon enough it'll sprout, and then we'll be breathing it in.'

I took the shot glasses from him.

'I think you've had too much.'

Inside, his other cats stared at me with gibbous eyes.

I ran into Mo on the way back to the flat. She was sat on the bottom step on the third floor, tossing a can of spray paint from one hand to another. In front of her, busy drying on the walls, was another one of her pieces. The same words.

'We're getting closer, I think.' She didn't even turn to look at me. I always did have a way of announcing my presence. 'I know what's going on, and I know how to stop it.'

She turned to me, tears in her eyes. 'They want us all to go, that's it. That's all it is. Do you have any idea what they've done?'

I shook my head. Above us, a plane flew low, the noise of the engines piercing the sounds of night in the block. After that, anything would sound peaceful, or conspiratorial.

'You know,' she said, pointing at her words on the wall, 'first saw that when I was little, over on a fence near the bus stop. It's a bar now, or an estate agents, I can't remember. There it was in faded paint, *King of This*. Someone's house that was on. I had to use it. Had to be mine. When I wrote those words, when I sprayed them on the walls, I was in control. This here is mine. This spot is where I am King.'

'Whose house was it? Who wrote the original?'

'That's the thing. A few weeks after I first started using it, I got off the bus and I walked past the house, and there it was on the fence. Brand new lick of paint. *No parking in front of this sign*. That's all it fucking said.'

She stood up and walked across to the balcony. I followed her and we both looked out across the courtyard.

'I know what they're doing. Trying to get us gone.'

'No one's trying to make us leave Mo. It's just kids. Just kids messing about.'

'I'm telling you, they're trying to make us leave. I've been out to the park. I've seen their words. Burned into the trees. They're doing this to us and that's why I'm writing my words, because these words have power, same as theirs.'

Outside the doorway to one of the other blocks, a couple of guys leaning against the wall shared a cigarette; tinny music played from one of their phones.

'I think you need to let the police handle it. I don't know what you saw, but it's just words. That's all. I know you're having fun and all, but you're taking this too far now Mo.'

'Ty.' She drifted off for a moment, trying to think of what to say. 'What if there were words you could write somewhere and you knew if you wrote them that your dad would be better?'

'But there aren't.'

'But what if there was?'

One of the men in the doorway stubbed his cigarette out on the floor with his foot, and the group disappeared in, taking the music with them. I'd never seen the courtyard so quiet.

Mo wiped the tears from her eyes. I could tell she was desperate to solve this. Everyone around the block was, me included. But what Mo was talking about, it didn't make any sense. Her and her lot were just out looking for someone to blame. If not some loner on the block, then the police, or some blokes in suits in some distant building trying to tear us all down. I thought she was just after blood. Maybe this was going down to a murky depth somewhere that she wouldn't be able to come back from.

'We've lived here all our lives, haven't we?' I said.

'Yeah, we have, but Ty, I'm scared about—'

'Just shut your eyes a second, like that. Tell me, what's right in front of us now?'

'East Block, I guess.'

'Yeah, and which lights are on, right now?'

'Paul probably; Tim and Ellen will have the TV on, but no lights. Oh, and up on the fifth floor, that flat no one lives in, bedroom light will be on too.'

I didn't even need to look. She was right.

'You know what that means? We've been here all our lives, and this place will always be here.'

Mo looked out at the buildings, and her eyes glazed over. As though she was looking through them. As though they weren't even there.

'You know what it means, Ty? It means fuck all.' And she turned and left me there.

Dad was too sick, they said. Could I be trusted to look after him twenty-four seven? I didn't know, and that was the honest truth. He needed round the clock care, and whilst there might be some money somewhere to help, it would end up costing me. I'd need to go home, they said, and think about my options.

When I went into his room, he was sat on the edge of the bed. It looked like he'd had the briefest of thoughts about getting up and going somewhere, but he'd gotten stuck. Frozen in the middle of a decision. He was clutching a plastic baby in his hand and when I asked the nurse about it, where it came from, why he had it, she just shrugged.

'He likes it,' she said, 'so just let him be. If you try and take it away, he'll lash out. He's done it to all of us on shift.' There were nods of agreement from several nurses at the desk.

I sat with him for a while and I thought about explaining everything to him: how I couldn't afford it, how he couldn't go back to the flats. I'd have to go too. Move somewhere cheaper. But when I opened my mouth, I realised just how far gone he was. Mo was wrong. Words don't have any power. Certainly not over someone who doesn't understand them.

I hugged him, whispering a meaningless *sorry* in his ear, and I left.

On the way home I thought about selling up and leaving. It was all I could do, and the way things were going at the flats, it would be better to leave now than see what happened.

They found Mo that morning. She was in the middle of the courtyard, blindfolded. A melted candle in her hand. Scrawled in blood next to her was her tag. *King of This.* Tape had cordoned off the courtyard by the time I got back, and the police were doing flat searches. I stood down there and I looked up at the railings and the bars, at the officers moving their way silently across them, and as they did I saw the buildings change. I saw them shift and lose their colour. The white tent surrounding her body was the brightest spot in the whole block.

'This place is going to the pits,' one of the officers said as he walked past me. 'They should just go ahead and knock the whole damned thing down. Rebuild. Start over.'

His partner agreed. 'Ask me, the rate they're going, give them five years and they'll have all killed each other.' Above, stood on the balcony looking down, was Desmond. A small black cat tiptoed along the rail next to him, wrapping its tail around his neck.

He seemed as though he didn't want to talk, though he invited me in all the same. We sat in his living room as cats paraded through silently.

'She liked you,' I told him.

'No, no. She thought I was just another old bastard waiting to die up here. I liked her though. Mo had ambition, more than any other folk in the blocks.'

I swigged from the bottle of cheap beer he'd handed me and looked at Desmond. His eyes had thinned, and he stared right at me. I couldn't tell whether what he'd said had been praise for her, or an insult to me.

'She said she was close to finding out who killed Gizmo. Said she'd seen something in the park. Carvings I think.'

'Don't doubt that for a second. Sharp mind on her. Saw what was there between the cracks.'

There wasn't much left to say. Not about Gizmo, not about my dad, and not about Mo. After something like what had happened, people would leave. That's just how it was. Some people like Desmond would stay. I could see it now: all of the flats torn down; new developments springing up left, right and centre; gold plated young professionals moving in on Daddy's money; and right there smack bang in the middle of it all, where a nice Swedish-designed playground should be, Desmond's flat, ten storeys up, teetering on a stalagmite of our old bedrooms and kitchens, our bathrooms and wardrobes, and right there in the middle of all *that*, red spray paint spelling out her words. *King of This*. Maybe, if that ever did come about, those words would have a power to them.

I put my bottle down on the table. A large tabby with one eye nudged my knee until I tickled her behind the ear.

'We'll find whoever did this.' I couldn't have sounded weaker if I'd tried.

'No, you won't.'

I got up and waded through the cats that littered the flat. When I got to the door, I turned and said, 'See you around'. But Desmond didn't move from his chair.

There were those who left out of fear. Gang violence they said. That's what got her killed. No parent wants their kid growing up in a place like that. Others found their rents hiked up. Priced out of a one-bed damp ridden shithole.

For me it was easy: they came round, a smiling woman in a business suit who shook my hand and said a word. A word that meant Dad could get the care he needed. That I could relocate and stop worrying about the mortgage payments that had gone unpaid for so many months. There were holdouts of course. There would always be holdouts. But they would find a way.

On the last day, I carried the final box out to the van I'd hired and I looked up at the tenth floor of Desmond's block.

He wasn't there, but I could still feel his eyes burning into me. He had eyes like a cat. The kind that you could feel watching you, without knowing where from, or why. Then, in the darkness, behind the railing, I could see the glistening of wet paint. Thick red letters daubed across the door of Desmond's flat. I could make out the K at the start, and the S at the end, and in the window I saw the face of a cat peering out at me.

For the first two miles as I drove away from there, I could feel it watching.

|Hunting by the River|

~

It's her eighteenth birthday and since she's his sister, he thought he'd head home and surprise her. Grabbing a bunch of flowers from a store in Manchester Piccadilly station, he walks across the city. It's still early, and he shares the streets with bleary-eyed tourists, dawn commuters and the sleeping homeless. He'd forgotten how the air felt in the city he grew up in: grey and wet, even on the sunniest of days. He's missed that.

So much of the city has changed since his last visit. It feels alien to him, and the pockets that remain are small safe havens of relief. His mum had always called it a city under construction, and it's as true now as it ever had been; looking up he spots cranes on the horizon. When he was old enough to come into the centre on his own, it had been the Arndale they were rebuilding after the bomb; now though, it was housing. Glass blocks of flats squeezed into every space. The skyline changed so often he could barely remember what it looked like.

He crosses Deansgate and turns down the road toward Salford.

The key he'd had since he was twelve still works, and even before he opens the door he can smell home, something so comforting and so impossible to describe in any other terms.

In the living room, his mum sits watching daytime TV, sunk into an armchair. When she sees him, she smiles briefly before bursting into tears.

'Jesus, Mum, it's just me.' He drops the flowers, runs over and hugs her.

Between tears she says, 'She's gone again.'

Kirsty left in the night. She's done it before. The last time, he recalls, was when she was thirteen. They'd found her a few days later in a squat out in Oldham, sigils etched into her skin with her school compass. There had been more since he'd left.

'The last time was a week ago,' his mum says, sipping a cup of tea he'd made her. 'I tried the police, but they know us. We're a faff to deal with and they know she comes back.'

'She will come back then?'

'Something feels different Lee, don't know what, but this isn't like the other times.'

'I'll find her. It'll be like before.'

His mum nods, staring down at her mug. He's never seen her this bad before, her face pink and pained, eyes squeezed small. As though she's trying to keep the world out of her head. He leans over and puts his hand on hers.

,We'll get her back. We always do.'

He doesn't know the city as well as he used to. It's ebbing from him, everything that tied him to this place vanishing piece by piece.

'Who's she hang out with these days?'

Lee finds the shop, nestled out beyond the university, near Rusholme. Places up that way feel hidden, and this is no different. He almost walks right past it. It's a newsagents, though he knows it isn't really. Terry, the bloke who runs it, had a nice line in coke back when Lee went clubbing. The shop has moved a few times since then, used to be up near the library till some private landowner came and bought up the ground beneath them. Now he's here, sandwiched between restaurants on Curry Mile.

Terry doesn't remember much, or at least he says he doesn't. She bought from him for a while, a bit of weed here and there, once or twice some pills. Nothing too drastic.

'Can't say I thought much of the lad she was with. Too old for a lass like her.'

His name is Nathan. Lee doesn't get a surname from Terry, but he gets an address. An estate over in Wythenshawe. No one knows for sure how long Kirsty's been with him. Terry delivered stuff to him once or twice.

It's a cul-de-sac, ringed with houses. Practically every one of them the same. In the middle of the day it's quiet – most people at work, kids at school. Driveways lie empty. Scaffolding is stacked against one property that he passes, builders chatting with drinks. They take no notice of him.

What is he planning on doing? He isn't sure. Knock on the door? Break a window? Try and find a spare key under a mat somewhere? He'd bet a tenner that none of those would work.

Lee finds number three. It stands out amongst the others. The front window is boarded up, though the glass appears to be intact. The grass in the front garden is overgrown, and a horrible smell is coming from the piled-up binbags lying against the hedge in front of the property. He glances at the upstairs window. The curtains are drawn and the lights are off.

Fuck it. He knocks on the door and waits.

There's no sound from the house. If she knew he was coming, she'd have found somewhere else to stay.

In the corner of his eye he spots a gap in the boards on the window. Inside he can just about make out the living room. It's dark, and it takes a moment for his eyes to register everything. A small coffee table sits in the centre of the room, wax melted into it from candles that have been placed all around it. They've been burned down so much that they're barely there anymore. On the table, spread out and stuck by the wax, is a map of Manchester. Thick black lines etched into it with charcoal. He recognises some of the places that he can make out from here: the town hall, the old cinema on Oxford Road, the Arndale.

There's writing on the walls, illegible scrawls. Lee remembers finding Kirsty that day years ago. Bloodied arms with symbols scarred into them.

What is she planning?

The next day he heads to The Koffee Pot for breakfast. He has an urge to immerse himself in the city, in the places he used to go. The Koffee Pot has moved. It's somewhere up a road in the Northern Quarter now, no longer resident on Stevenson Square. Doesn't matter, it still feels the same inside. He takes a seat by the window.

After a few sips of coffee, he notices someone sitting opposite him. A young lad, no more than about thirteen. He's skinny as fuck, baseball cap pulled down over his eyes and he doesn't look up at Lee.

'Alright Lee?' he says in Kirsty's voice.

'Who's this you've come to me as?'

'Does it really matter?' The boy fiddles with a napkin, doesn't look up. 'I know you're looking for me, and I'd like you to stop. I'm okay.'

'You're so okay that you've come to chat in someone else's body. Is that okay?'

The boy looks up at Lee, and he can almost see her eyes, witchy and hazel, somewhere behind the boy's own.

'Mum's worried sick.'

He jumps at someone banging on the window. The boy doesn't react at all. He turns to spot a stag do barreling past down the street, and when he turns back, the boy has his head down again.

'Thanks for giving a shit, but I don't need rescuing. Not this time.'

'I went to Nathan's. I saw the map.'

What have you got planned? he doesn't ask.

'Yeah, I guessed that was you. Bloody Terry, right? I told Nate not to trust him. Doesn't matter. We're long gone now.'

Lee reaches out to the boy, feeling as though he can reach through, find his sister and pull her out of the body, back into reality. The boy shuffles back.

'Please don't. Might wake him up, then we can't chat. I've missed you Lee. You've not called in a bit.'

'Been busy.'

'London's changed you, you Southern cunt.' He can hear her laugh, though the boy's mouth doesn't change expression.

'I noticed this place has moved.'

'About a year ago I think. Cocktail place moved in. The city's different. Don't you feel it? Doesn't it make you sick?'

The boy looks around at the people sitting near them, suspicious. Lee looks around too, copying him, but not understanding why. A waitress comes over to take his mug but he clutches hold of it even though it's empty. The boy with Kirsty's voice hasn't ordered anything.

'I don't know what I feel Kirst, I've not been here for years, it doesn't feel like home anymore.'

'Exactly. Exactly. No more mithering about. Things have got to change, Lee. They have to. It's got to go back to how it all was.'

'But that's not the city. It's just me. Places change, people change, sometimes at the same time. Doesn't mean anything bad. Doesn't mean anything. Just means stuff evolves.'

'You're wrong Lee.'

The boy grabs hold of his wrist and his eyes roll into his head. The whites stare back for just a moment, then the colour returns and he eyes Lee with suspicion.

'The fuck's going on?'

He goes back to his mum's empty handed, and she cries on his shoulder for a little while before he makes her a brew, then they sit with the TV on in the background, talking about Kirsty.

When Lee went to look for her all those years ago, the first time she disappeared, he remembered the stories, little snatches from her friends, sometimes from strangers. The names they called her. Nicknames whose origins he could never pin down. He saw those same nicknames on the bus months later, etched into the metal headrests, scored into the glass on the window, and he winced when he saw them. Lies, tales and rumours had lead him to the squat out in Oldham. How she'd fallen in with the scally fuckers who lived in that mouldy, broken home he'd never known, but he'd dragged her out by her arm. She'd called him all sorts but he was keeping her safe, he was doing the right thing. None of the others in that place had tried to stop him.

His mum had been so relieved. They sat vigilant all night in case she tried to leave again.

Tonight, they sit together the way they did all of those years ago, hopeful that she will walk down the stairs as though nothing has happened.

The sightings come in few and far between. Texts saying she'd been seen walking through The Printworks in tattered clothes, bleeding. No, make that lying prone in the middle of Deansgate, speaking in tongues. Another one said she'd been lying low in Heaton Park, sleeping rough in a tent she'd stolen from the Trafford Centre. But none of the leads come to anything, and all of them contradict one another. Kirsty, for a few days, exists across the whole city all at once.

Then there's a sighting of her in-between the cities. A patch of wasteland just beyond the Irwell. She'd been standing there in the rain, arms aloft, soaked to her skin. Another boy there too, probably Nate. She was screaming at the sky. He was reading from a book. That had been three days earlier, according to the friend who rang him. It frustrates Lee, how long it takes for news to come his way, but at least it *is* news. That's something.

He walks there one morning, just ten minutes from his mum's place, just ten minutes from where Kirsty had lived. There had been something here, years ago. He remembers something vague: a hotel, an estate? Something he'd never dared enter. Now, whatever had stood there has been demolished, a mound of dirt stacked at the verge, next to the road. There's no building equipment, no sign of any presence there anymore. Just an empty patch of land that belongs to no one. Except that isn't true. He treads through dewey grass towards the centre, stumbling over rocks and holes where foundations and pipes were supposed to be laid, and looks up at the sky. Grey clouds shift across Manchester, a light rain falls, and he dreams of his sister, standing there, scarred and screaming. Up ahead of him, rising up fast and different, is the city. The towering hotels and old warehouses dulled and washed out in the rain. *This is what she had seen* he thinks, shaking himself out of the past, focusing on the here and now.

This is why she had been so angry. So scared.

A woman leaves the block of flats next to the wasteland and stares at him. For a moment he's convinced it's Kirsty. Another one of her tricks. But the woman turns and walks away quick, lifting her coat above her head to protect her from the rain.

He knows then that he will see her everywhere.

Nate's body washes up at the Deansgate locks two days later. The smokers outside of Revolution spot him. There's no sign of injury and he's reported in the papers as a 'reveller' who fell. It takes a call from Terry to tell Lee that this is the bloke.

'You should quit,' he tells Lee. 'She doesn't want to be found.'

But there's something about Terry's voice that doesn't sound right.

He doesn't go back down south, not right away. There will come a time when he'll have to, when his life down there will catch back up with him, but Manchester has a way of stalling time, keeping things still for longer than they should. He feels as though he's exhausting his moment of stillness, draining the goodwill of the city. There are days when he feels a haze fall over him, a thick mist coating him, and when it leaves he finds himself in a part of the city he doesn't recognise right away. He wakes up in the industrial estates of Trafford, under the pagoda in Chinatown, and halfway down Princess Parkway, passing cars honking at him. Then there are worse days, days when he feels he's in control of himself, days when he goes out looking for her still. Wandering the streets of the Northern Quarter he feels someone brush past him and whisper in his ear,

'What are you still doing here Lee?'

And he knows who it is, but when he turns around, the stranger who spoke to him is already walking away. He can't touch them. He knows what will happen and so there's no point. Some days, in cafes and shops, he'll see someone watching him and he'll know it's her, and he'll approach them, and say, 'Please Kirst, come home. Mum misses you.'

It's all he has left.

But their blank expressions tell him everything he needs to know, and he apologises, and pays for his coffee.

Lee sleeps at his mum's place, in Kirsty's room. It's that or the settee. At night, when he can't sleep, he walks from the house, away from Salford, towards Manchester. In Manchester, they call Salford *the other city*, but to him, it's the other way around. Manchester: a strange, enlarged reflection of the place he grew up. He skirts around the edges of it, as though he's looking for a door, and he crosses Bridge Street over the Irwell.

Dawn is coming up, an eggy cream blasting the sky beyond the clouds. It should be cold but he doesn't feel it. The walk has kept him warm enough. He follows the river as it runs parallel to Deansgate, bordering Manchester like a moat, keeping on it for as long as he can until it shifts direction and runs away, twisting around and flowing towards Bolton and Pendle. Witch country.

He recalls the lines on the map in the house, and he looks at the way the river flows. Has it always flowed this way?

And he notices things within it, bobbing on the river, being carried away from the city. At first it's just bricks, shopping carts, bottles. But then, the detritus grows, and he sees everything there: bicycles, entire streets and houses, crumbled and broken and being flushed out. Jagged blocks of tarmac rolling in the current, knocking into road signs, and bulldozing over high-vis jackets which float on the surface of the water. Some building equipment floats past, and Lee notices the hook of a crane sinking slowly into the depths.

He sees the first person. They are dead, bobbing on the surface the way Nate probably did. *Just another reveller,* he thinks briefly. More people come next, so many people. Some are dead, drowned and grey and bloated, but some are alive, desperately looking up at him to save them, clawing at the edges of the river, their bloodied fingernails breaking on the brick.

He watches as they are carried out of Manchester towards witch country. Then he turns, and starts walking into the current, back towards the city, towards her city.

|Flotsam|

~

The arrival

No one could recall the storm, though it is true to say that a storm had passed. The evidence was there, carried on a calm wind and the smudged grey sky like a poorly erased mistake in pencil. A curious amount of detritus had blown through the town also: a single bloodied shoe, a small doll with too many limbs to be human, a rusted bayonet (perhaps not rust, but rather ancient blood). Amongst the artefacts was discovered an iron helmet cleaved in two, its jagged edges cauterised and blackened.

The creature had arrived during the storm. It had erupted from the depths of the ocean, fatally wounded, and had hauled itself on to the pebbled beach where it had gasped a final, inhuman breath and died, leaving behind a trail of its blood, thicker than oil, which traced its path from the ocean and spooled around in a whirlpool from where it had originated.

What the creature looked like

There was never a consensus in the town on precisely what the creature looked like. The things that most agreed on – thick black tentacles, no eyes, a ridge of spine-like hair across its back – were refuted by others who saw bright colours, scales and too many eyes. The children in the village were not scared of it, not like some of us adults. They would freely walk close by and play around it, sometimes building it a home out of sand, or redirecting the route of the tide to create a protective moat around the thing. What did they see when they looked at it? Something friendly, or perhaps something so monstrous it could not be processed by childlike minds.

For some of us, just looking at the creature brought on terrible headaches almost instantly; headaches so painful that they caused bright colours to dance across your eyes. At night, those who had seen the creature dreamt dreadful things, waking up in a cold sweat, practically feverish. It would pass quickly, and after that you learned to look away.

There were a select few, though, whom the creature did not appear to affect. Mrs Bradley was the most prominent, though she was always like that at any event in the village. Mrs Bradley made the best cakes for the school fundraiser, she won village garden of the year, and she grew the biggest cauliflowers around. Everyone knew Mrs Bradley, or rather, everyone *had* to know Mrs Bradley, and it was as though that piece of village lore had passed on subconsciously to the creature itself. When she approached it on that first day, whilst the rest of us staggered back from the pain in our heads, she was unaffected. She touched it. Stroked it. I saw an oily black residue coat her hand, dripping onto the pebbles below.

She said, 'It has been brought here for a reason, and we must devour it.' The way she muttered it to herself, it felt like an affirmation.

Mrs Bradley argues her case

There was some debate at first. Most of the village gathered in the Scout hut by the creek, squashed into the space. It felt clandestine, as though we were hiding from this dead thing on the beach. The local councillor, Mr Peabody, was angry that this meeting even had to be called in the first place. Why should we, on Mrs Bradley's say-so, eat the creature that had washed up from some unknown place? There were stories, Brian Hargreaves the butcher said, about fish who were caught, cooked and eaten, who contained within them immense poisons. Did Mrs Bradley wish to kill us all?

The thing should rot, claimed several people. It should be left there to rot and die. Maybe then the headaches and dreams would end. It should be forgotten about. We should not speak of it again. Cast it into history.

But Mrs Bradley was adamant. 'It has come here for a reason. You all fear it and look how it treats you. I don't fear it. I admire it.'

Then, someone suggested, if Mrs Bradley is so keen to eat the creature, would she be willing to be the first to consume it?

She would do it gladly. She would be so proud to be the first.

What did people dream when they saw the creature?

The cosmos, spiralling out and out and out, ad infinitum. Sparks of life exploding in interstellar clusters. A feeling of dread, of sinking into nothing. Facts and knowledge that you cannot understand and so they sit at the edge of your mind, on the tip of your tongue, waiting just out of reach for you. And then, the inhuman screams of something vast, echoing across the universe, touching signals from asteroids and moons like radar. It is a scream without emotion, but it instils a kind of fear within you which you have never felt before in your life. Louder than anything you have ever heard. How small you feel. How insignificant. How utterly pointless.

How many could touch the creature?

At first just three: Mrs Bradley, Ms Hobson the baker, and Mr Stoakley the farmer. Just three to begin with, although over time, there were more.

Mrs Bradley eats the first piece

She didn't cook it. She ate the thing raw.

After it was agreed that she would be the first to eat the creature, she retrieved a carving knife from her kitchen and made her way to the beach. Some of the villagers followed her, despite the onslaught of pain from the creature. They watched as she took the knife to the creature, slicing a small piece of one tentacle. It came away gently, slipping from the rest of the body and splattering into the bucket Mrs Bradley had prepared for it. A little oily black blood dribbled from the wound.

Do any of the people who were present recall the creature shifting and twitching when she cut into it? No.

Mrs Bradley took the bucket and sat on the edge of the seafront, looking out across the horizon. The trail of blood still floated on top of the water like a scar. She plunged her hand into the bucket and took out the piece of the creature. Almost immediately she tore into it with her teeth, ripping its flesh apart. The oily black substance stained her mouth and chin, dripping down onto her clothes. She smiled when she ate it. She smiled like she had never smiled before.

When did Mrs Bradley die?

At 142, she lived the longest.

Another meeting called

No ill effects were observed in Mrs Bradley, who continued her day to day life in the usual manner. Her vegetables grew large and impressive and she tended to her garden obsessively. However, there did appear to be a marked change in how she moved, how she carried herself. It was as if she floated, or knew some piece of impossible information. Everyone saw that change in her. Everyone wanted a part of it. It was the creature that did it. Eating a piece of it had given her a kind of revelation, and why should the rest of the village not be privy to the same thing?

Mr Peabody brought the meeting to order, but almost immediately Mr Stoakley interrupted him. Mrs Bradley had been permitted to eat the creature. Mrs Bradley had seen something. Why shouldn't the rest of us get the chance?

Not all of us felt the pull of the creature. Not at this time. But after Mrs Bradley ate the tentacle there were more who could look upon it without experiencing terrible pain. Fewer dreamers, screaming in the night.

It was decided that each man and woman would make their own choice. If they wished to eat the creature then they might do so, providing they took only a slice. If they wished to leave it be, then so be it.

The questions nobody asked

Where did the creature come from?

What kind of storm leaves a trace, but cannot be recalled?

What kind of creature wants to be consumed?

A queue forms

They brought their knives from home, scythes from the wheat fields, Swiss Army knives shining red in the sun from the pockets of their Scout leader uniforms. They didn't surround the creature and tear it apart. No, they formed a queue, winding its way up the beach, straddling the wall at the back and flowing up the steps to the promenade. It snaked past the fish and chip shop on the corner, past the B&B and up towards the high street. Mrs Bradley paraded up and down, shaking everyone's hands. She didn't say anything, didn't have to. It was all in her eyes. Welcome, her eyes said. The first day of the mass consumption of the creature was a glorious day.

The holdouts notice a change

It was not immediately apparent. Life continued as normal. There were a few hundred or so who chose to abstain from eating the creature. Walking down the promenade, their heads throbbed and they couldn't help but turn to look at the corpse lying on the beach, slices of flesh missing, so that it resembled something even more alien that it had previously. It was not just in its fractured body that they saw a difference. There was an emptiness to the town.

In their nightmares they saw the villagers who took part in the eating. The oily blood from the creature cascading from their mouths. Not just that black, viscous liquid but the pieces of the creature itself, slipping from their mouths, regurgitating itself. The pieces came together in the middle of a supernova of light.

When spoken to, the villagers who ate the creature were cordial. They took part in small talk and asked questions about family members: How is Uncle John? Did little Sally get her silver in swimming? Is the kitchen going to be finished by Easter? But to the holdouts there was something missing. It felt like a performance.

It drove them away, one by one.

What of the detritus?

After the storm, the bayonet, shoe, doll and helmet were all immediately taken to the library to be photographed and retained for historical record. They remained there during the consumption. No photographs were ever taken and, as with all things, no record was made. Instead, they were locked away. The relationship between these objects was never discussed or considered, and the whereabouts of the other shoe in the pair (a right) was not pondered.

They touch the creature

They stood around it one morning, all of those who had eaten a part of the creature. The remaining villagers who hadn't tasted the innards of the thing on the beach caught sight of it on their way to work, or on the school run. Hundreds of them surrounding the corpse, hand in hand. Mrs Bradley was right there, and though the circle did not have a start or end point, it seemed as though she was at the head of it. The day was quiet, no cars rumbling along the high street, no clinking of empty milk bottles being picked up. All that could be heard was the calm slosh of the tide, and the odd hollowness of pebbles shifting beneath feet.

Somewhere in the distance, across the horizon and far from the eyes of the villagers, a ship's horn rumbled in the air. Those watching the group encircling the creature turned to look for the source of the sound. Those with their hands clasped did not move.

It was as though they approached the creature, closing in on it. But they did not move so that couldn't be true. It was just as likely to suggest that the creature, dead as it was, expanded to fit the space created by the circle of hands. That it fattened itself. What remained of its skin rippled around it, following the ring of consumers. The people surrounding it shuddered momentarily, as though being caught off guard whilst standing on a moving train, then righted themselves and offered no further movement. All save Mrs Bradley. Her face was an assiduous mask of concentration, but for the glimmer of a smile, for just a moment.

The creature expanded to touch each of the people, pushing itself against them, bulging out through the gaps between their hands, the spaces below and above their arms. One lone tentacle escaped between someone's legs, then whipped itself back into the fray just as quickly.

Those who had not consumed a part of the creature fought the vicious headaches they experienced, some practically blinded by the pain. They fought so they could watch. They felt a need to witness this that had nothing to do with its strangeness. This appeared strange to no one. No, this felt wholly expected.

What did Mrs Bradley die of?

Unknown causes. She was cold to the touch, and stiff as a bone. No blood was discovered either outside her body nor within it, though a tiny patch of oil close to her body was noted in the coroner's report.

Inside the circle

It breathed its first in an age, taking in one or two primitive minds and expelling the scraps back out into their bodies. There they were: pieces of it, inside them all. Digested and absorbed into skin and fat and blood. There was a piece of it careening around, hidden in some minuscule vein. Another breath. The sweet taste of a soul. Memories flooded through it. Unknowable things. A party by a river, the wind picking up a tablecloth. A sudden rush indoors at the first sparks of rain. It searched within for something more filling. There: a horrible thought, an anxious woman pacing in the corridor of a hospital. The news will be bad. She knows it will. That would do. It released what it hadn't devoured, broken and piecemeal though it was. All the while it grew, found strength that it forgot it had.

The library is opened

Mr Peabody ran from the events on the beach. He knew each and every one of the people in that circle and he watched briefly as they shuddered and lost themselves to the creature. There were shards of glass in his head, scratching at his mind. A pain like no other he had ever felt in his life. Turning tail, he abandoned them to the thing that had washed up. What had happened to his town? He thought back to the day after the storm that he could not recall, when the creature appeared. His head splintered as though a bullet had pierced it. A pain that stopped him dead in his tracks.

But he recalled the detritus that washed up in the town the same night. Recalled where it was being stored.

Mr Peabody ran.

The streets were empty. Everyone was at the beach. Those who didn't eat, watching, those who ate, participating. Mr Peabody raced down the high street, passing open stores with no workers, dogs tied to lampposts, barking for owners who were far from them. From inside The Railway Arms he caught the sound of a football game being watched by no one, and heard the trickling of a tap still running. But he did not stop. He felt a burning racing across his chest, tightening his veins. Like whatever kept him running was seeping from him, being devoured piece by piece. The library could not be far.

Glass scattered on the floor when he broke the window. He found himself surprised by it. Not the act of destruction so much as the evidence left behind. *Did I do that?* he found himself asking as he clambered through the gap into the library.

The crowd attempts to watch

The pebbles all around the circle shifted, as though being trodden on. Pain cascaded through all of the non-eaters, though they could not look away. The thing that had washed up on their shores roared in their minds. All of them. A terrible indecipherable speech that tore through them. Some were knocked to the floor, others staggered back. One or two stood their ground. No one dared get close to the events taking place at the shoreline. Those who formed the circle clutched each other's hands, but their bodies appeared limp. All except for Mrs Bradley. Mrs Bradley's smile was as terrible as the creature itself. She stared right at the creature. Smiling. What was the creature saying to them? What was it saying to her? Whatever it was, to those watching, it felt like the end of all things.

A bayonet, a doll, a helmet, and a shoe

They were hers once. Torn from her as she dragged the thing into the rift. The doll she had been given by her mother, so many years ago. So long that she couldn't even recall it not being in her life. It was apt then that in that moment she would lose it.

On the beach

Mr Peabody sprinted towards the circle. The closer he got to the creature the more the pain in his head intensified. Pain unlike anything he had ever experienced. As though his brain was pouring out through his ears. But it wouldn't stop him. Brandishing the bayonet, he ran forward towards the eaters. The creature, a writhing mass, was a negative space in front of him, an absence of light. It had nearly engulfed all of the circle now, close to breaking free. Where a part of it had been eaten, it was regrown, the wounds zipped together and closed. Tentacles sneaked around the area, combing the beach, lifting pebbles. A screaming sounded in his ears and Mr Peabody understood what it was. The creature was laughing. Laughing at his attempts to do what he was trying to do. No matter. He reached the edge of the circle and, raising the bayonet above his head, he leapt forward, toward the screaming thing.

Mr Peabody falls

The bayonet stuck in the creature and Mr Peabody fell. He clutched the doll in his hand, but his hand was weak and he could not hold on to it much longer. The creature screamed again and he thought *It's in my head, and how much more of this can I take?* But it was not in his head this time. A great shockwave passed through the circle, breaking clasped hands, showering the promenade with pebbles, and washing the tide out. Mr Peabody felt a wetness against his cheek and he touched it, bringing back a handful of blood. *The doll is a curious thing*, he thought. *So many arms.*

So many arms.

Mrs Bradley wishes for death

At 142, don't we all? She felt a change after the creature left. A rushing of something inside of her. None of the other eaters experienced it. She understood in that moment that it was because she was the first. She was trusted and she had been gifted something. The others, they became husks. Something had been taken from all of them. Mr Stoakley went back to running his farm, but he could never keep an animal alive for more than a couple of months. He could be seen sometimes, standing on the beach, weeping. Others who had been in that circle could be seen there sometimes too. Mr Hobson often went there and walked across the shore, picking up pebbles and checking under them. Mrs Bradley felt none of this, except that deep within her there was a terrible longing. She didn't go back to the beach, not for any of the many decades she remained in the village. The children who saw her named her Grandma Ankou and crossed the road to avoid her, lest she drag them to hell with her at night. It was curious as to how the stories they told about her took something from her each time she heard them. As though the children were carving little pieces of her, and eating them raw.

|Stink Pit|

The car is a rental, and though Alex tried to pay in cash, they only took card. That's that part of the plan fucked, thinks Lucy when he tells her. The others don't seem to care so much. They're fired up: Oppo has a leg twitch that comes alive when he's excited. Rob's taken to fiddling with the lighter he keeps in his pocket, the one that Oppo gave him the night before they set off.

'Why'd they call you that again?' asks Alex from the driver's seat, even though everyone in the car has heard the story before over clandestine drinks in The Bleeding Wolf.

'Army's fucked,' Oppo says, 'full of fascists and Tories—'

'Same difference,' Rob chimes in next to him.

Oppo grins, 'It wasn't like that for me. Joined because of my old man. He was straight in at sixteen, never left. Died on the Galahad in the Falklands, burned alive. Don't think I was ever cut out for it, but I joined anyway. It was like, that was my way into him, you know? To understand him. But I couldn't get on board with it, could I? They said 'jump', I said 'fuck off'. So they called me Oppo. Then it's about the little things. Someone gets a round in, 'oh, didn't get Oppo a pint, just got him a coke, 'cos he likes to be different.' Then you worry about who's got your back, who you can trust.'

'You trust us lot though, right Oppo?' Lucy leans over from the passenger side and squeezes his knee.

'Yeah, well enough.'

The car ploughs through a thick morning fog, dew coating the windows. The woods hold an eerie silence at this time in the morning. Last thing they want to be doing is disturbing the peace so early, but they have to, if they're to get this sorted before the hunt kicks off.

Rob brought Oppo in to all of this. They started drinking together at the Wolf a few months ago, the two of them just a couple of lost, lonely blokes stood next to each other at the bar. A few dirty jokes, and some slightly aggressive political fights, and they found themselves perfect company. To Rob, Oppo seemed to be looking for something that he couldn't quite put his finger on. When Rob mentioned what he got up to at the weekends, that was when Oppo got excited.

'Fucking pricks,' he'd said at the first proper meeting of the four of them. Lucy had some of the pictures she'd taken the last time they'd tried to sabotage a hunt. They were too late, or word had got out.

'They think they can just get away with it.'

'They can,' Alex replied, 'that's the problem. That's where we come in. You too, if you're up for it. Christ knows we could do with some army training on our side.'

Rob had been doing this for as long as he could remember, used to arrange the buses that took groups of sabs all around the north: Yorkshire, Prestwich, even out to Wales sometimes. Mostly grouse hunts, the occasional pheasant. But it was getting harder. Too often they'd get there to find that whatever hunt they'd been after had rearranged, planned a bye day or rain had called it all off. The worst times, they'd park up and hear the familiar buzz of a drone hovering somewhere above them; that's when they knew the police were coming for them. Once, at a court hearing for an old friend, Rob watched as a member of the hunt said to the solicitor questioning him that they'd had a tip off from a local officer that sabs were on the way.

It was all a game to them, and Rob needed to up his.

Oppo learned from them just as much as they learned from him. They showed him how to spray coverts to confuse the foxhounds, how to set false trails and pre-beat the area. Classic stuff really. Oppo brought in the tactical side of things, showed them how to cover their tracks. Hide their identities.

After the first meeting, at Oppo's place, they met in the open, at a table in the Wolf, but they wore sports gear. If they travelled anywhere, they would do it by rental. He was smart and organised. They all got the sense that the next time they went out, they'd have a fair amount more success than before.

It had been Alex who mentioned it quietly, when Oppo had gone for a piss.

'You think he might be a cop?'

'Seriously?' Lucy wasn't having it, and neither was Rob for that matter. He knew the stories; they all did. A guy called Mike who'd been going out with a mate of theirs for years turned out to be undercover, trying to get into the inner circle of a local Greenpeace branch.

'I trust him,' Rob said. 'What would they even want with us? Must cost a fortune to place someone undercover like that. Are we even worth investigating?'

'Rob's right,' Lucy said, 'there's barely any of us.'

That had been the extent of the conversation. It seemed enough for the lot of them. Chat moved on to the usual – Rob's mum's health, the lack of funding at Lucy's school and the state of the kids there. By the time Oppo came back, they were laughing about something or other, and the whole thing had been forgotten.

Anyway, Rob had been round Oppo's place, a few times, after they'd all been there, and that was normally a big no-no in the undercover world. It wasn't anything fancy, just a studio in the Northern Quarter, behind Odd Bar, but it felt like Oppo's home: couple of dirty dishes sitting in the kitchen, the same smell of stale smoke that hung around him (a holdover from the army where he got taught to smoke and keep calm with the best of them), Madchester posters blu-tacked to the walls, peeling off with damp. The two of them had finished off the best of a crate of beer and played god knows how many rounds of Tekken that night, and Oppo hadn't once tried to ask questions about the sab side of things. It had just been – and Rob hated the word – banter.

The day rope bangers were Oppo's idea, so was the place to go. Lucy rented a Jeep and drove out to the countryside in the Cheshire wilderness to buy them. The way she told it, she'd gone fully undercover in the countryside alliance, donning a quilted gilet and a terrible posh accent.

'It'll be like, insurgent tactics and shit,' Oppo said, 'Buy a few of the bird scarer ropes, string them up around the woods and light them up. They burn for about half an hour each, so set them up to go off over an hour or so and that'll scare off any wildlife in the area. They'll all go to ground.'

They'd need to keep the ropes away from the ground to keep the dry and brittle leaves from catching, and they'd need to time it perfectly, but it was a good plan.

Fucking up the car rental isn't the end of the world, they decide. It only becomes a problem if someone discovers the car and jots down the number plate. Rob's worry comes from that day stood in the back of the court. The way the bloke from the hunt so brazenly admitted to the cops feeding them intel on the sabs. He never thought it was that bad, but there it was. What if they took the plate number and gave it to some mate working high up in the police? They'd be able to track the car down no problem, then it's just a hop, step and a jump away from linking the car to Alex, Alex to the rest of them.

The worry clings to him, but there's nothing they can do now. It's 5a.m. and they're already at the edge of the estate. Alex finds a good spot to park the car, behind a spinney of oaks and far enough away from the roads that it would be difficult to spot. The covert is only a mile or so away, near to The George and Dragon, where they know the hunt is going to start from.

They walk in single file, Oppo at the back, monitoring things. Alex is up front.

'Sorry about the car,' he says to all of them, and none of them. He's already apologised umpteen times this morning.

'It'll be fine,' Rob says. 'If anything, we're being too precautionary, you don't need to worry so much.'

The ground is bone dry, thanks to weeks of horrible, cloying heat. Whatever was growing in the fields they cross is browned and dying. Somewhere distant, Rob hears the scream of a sheep, the rumble of a tractor.

Soon enough, the single file arrangement is lost. Rob catches up with Alex at the front whilst Lucy and Oppo share a cigarette.

'The story is always the same, isn't it?' Alex says.

'How do you mean?'

'With Oppo like, about his name, he never changes it.'

'Yeah, I know. What do you mean by that?'

'I mean Rob, it always stays the same, word for word,' he stops and looks dead at Rob, 'like it's rehearsed.'

Rob looks behind him at Oppo and Lucy. She's laughing at the punchline to some stupid joke. No, Alex is wrong. Suspicion is good, it's healthy, but he's wrong. The way they met, the things they've done together. The way Oppo just sort of hangs around, doesn't press for anything. If he was undercover he'd have wormed his way in more. If he was undercover he'd be with some other group, like Chris' lot over in Cumbria. They were the real fighters. One of Chris' lot had torn the earlobe off a pretty prominent Lord at a grouse hunt back in December. That was where the trouble was. Not here. No. Alex is wrong.

He hopes.

They find the covert beyond the field, a patch of woodland, bristling with dry, almost dead looking wych elms.

'Once the rook scarers go off, they should echo around this place pretty good,' says Oppo, removing his bag and opening it up. 'No real need to worry about where we put them, but spread them around a bit, just to be sure. And keep them up off the floor. We don't want to start any fires, do we?'

Lucy mock salutes him, 'Safety first sarge.'

They start setting the first rope up. Oppo climbs a nearby tree, finds a sturdy branch above head height, and shuffles along to the end of it. He ties one of the scarers around it, letting it dangle down.

'When we're ready, we'll light the bottom. Has a burn time of six hours this, and one of these,' he points at one of the shotgun shell-shaped bangers attached to rope, 'will go off every half hour or so.'

They make their way around the woodland, taking it in turns to clamber up the trees and attach one of the banger ropes. Rob hasn't climbed a tree since he was a kid. It feels oddly freeing. As he's tying the knot in his rope he looks down at Oppo, pouring coffee into paper cups for the rest of them. There's silence all around them. If something were to happen, Rob thinks, now is when it would. Before they lit the ropes, before the hunt even began. They'd be caught in the act right now before any damage was done. That there is silence can only mean Oppo is okay.

Then Lucy says, 'do you smell that?'

Rob climbs down. He holds his head up and sniffs the air. Yes, there it is, unmistakable and horrific. Death.

'It's coming downwind,' Oppo says and points to his left. 'Over there, I think.'

The four of them pick their bags up.

At the edge of the woodland, they cross a splintered tree trunk and wade through a low stream. The smell is getting worse, thick in the humid morning air. Rob pulls a headscarf up from around his neck to cover his nose and mouth.

They find it beneath the trunk of a tree, where the dried leaves have turned to a horrible mulch. Lucy turns away immediately, Alex holds his arms out in front of her as if to absorb the sight. Oppo... Rob doesn't see what Oppo does. Rob is far too busy trying to comprehend it.

II

There's an email sent around to everyone in the office that they can go home early, as a treat. Some of the team are going for a pint around the corner but Rob just wants to get home instead. The job is killing him, he can feel it somewhere deep inside of him. Literally, he thinks: the carcinogens he's inhaling coming into work, the diseases he's breathing in on public transport, the crap he winds up eating. But there's a part of him that also knows taking this job was the moment he gave it all up.

He knows the moment that the fire inside him died. The sense of right and wrong. He remembers so clearly marching against the war in 2003, how many thousands of people did that, knowing they were right, and what came of it? Nothing. It was all for nought.

What a shitshow.

When the ban came in a year later, they all saw it for what it was, a fiction. The hunts still carried on, and Rob saw from friends' statuses on Facebook, posts on forums he was still a member of, that the sabs were still out there. But he didn't have it in him to carry on. Whatever fight had been in him was gone. Now here he was. Once or twice he'd found himself trawling the usual groups online to find details of a hunt, a little piece of him tugging at his shirt to get him back out there.

Then there were the nightmares. In them, he walks through the covert tying rook scarers to the trees. Then he comes across the pit. It smells dead, the way it did that day, but he keeps on, stepping forwards into the blood red mud that coats the ground. He hears Lucy say, 'What is it? What the fuck is it?' And he can't answer. At first glance he'd say a fox, torn apart. Its burnt orange fur shredded and bloodied, exposing broken bones and punctured muscle. But where a fox's head would be, instead there was a brace of chicken heads, their eyes poked out and cauterised. In between them, reaching out towards him, fingers still grasping at life, a human hand.

He would wake, as always, in a horrible clammy sweat. A sweat that would cling to his back for days afterwards, and as it did so, it would carry with it that same stink of deadness.

He crosses the road by the Bridgewater Hall and passes the pub on the corner. Flowing beneath him is the canal. He remembers stories appearing in the paper every now and again, guys walking home drunk, falling in and drowning. Got so bad they used to think there was a serial killer afoot. No, it was just Manchester. On the other side of the road, the familiar rise and fall noises of afternoon drinkers on the locks. From where he's stood, he can't see them but he can hear them well enough. The ghosts of the city.

Further out, towards Moss Side where his flat is, it's all building sites. Cranes and scaffolding. Half of them boarded and shuttered. People haven't set foot in them in months. Maybe they wouldn't ever come back. He knew a couple from the old days who used to break into all sorts of abandoned places, document it all on camera. They'd post pictures from drowning underground stations, collapsed businesses, perfectly preserved apartments. Now, though, it was building sites. City under construction, who had said that to him? He had a memory of being sat in the Wolf one night, laughing stupidly at that.

Alex. It takes him the whole walk home to remember the name. He hasn't thought of Alex in years. Why hasn't he thought of Alex?

Never mind, it's the old days.

When he flicks the light on in his flat he notices the footprints, thick-soled and muddy, leading from the doorway into the living room.

'Hello?' he says, trying to be casual.

He takes a few steps forward. The living room light is off, but he can see the blueish flicker of the TV. Searching his pocket, he finds his keys and holds them in his hand, the blade of the doorkey sticking out between his fingers, the way he used to hold them when he was growing up.

The moment he steps into the living room he drops the keys from his hands. Oppo's lying on his sofa, crying gently. His head was shaved the last time Rob saw him; now, his long greasy hair sticks to his forehead, tangled up in his thick beard. Underneath the green waterproof, Rob can tell that he's skinny as anything. Whatever muscle there had been back in his army days has been decimated.

Mud dribbles down from Oppo to the rug, pooling there.

'Jesus Oppo. Jesus.'

Rob doesn't ask him anything, just grabs Oppo a glass of water from the kitchen and brings it back. He tips the glass up to his lips and pours some down his throat.

'Where've you been? I haven't seen you since—'

But he can't remember. Was it that day in the covert, with the rope scarers? When they reached the edge of the woodland and saw his nightmare? So much of that time after is adrift in his mind. How did they get back? Did they light the ropes?

Oppo retches and Rob helps him lift his head a little.

'Come on man, just a little bit of water, it'll help.'

He raises the glass to Oppo's lips again, and after he's taken a sip the backwash brings crumbs of soil. Oppo retches again, like he's going to throw up, and Rob instinctively slaps his back. He does it again, and again, and Oppo stretches his head up towards the ceiling, muscles in his neck tense. Something is stuck, lodged in there.

'Hold still,' Rob says, taking the same tone he'd take with a dog. 'Let me get at it.'

He tries to be delicate, but finds his fingers clumsily navigating what's left of Oppo's teeth, grasping for whatever it is that's in his throat. Then he feels it, the edge of something sharp and thin. Rob pulls at it, feeling it dislodge and give.

As the tip of it comes out of Oppo's mouth, Rob sees that it's a twig. No, more than that, because it keeps on coming, and the twig that he has hold of is attached to a branch. Leaves pop out between Oppo's teeth, tiny acorns still hanging between them. Blood stains the sharp ends where pieces of it have broken off inside him, scratched his throat and torn at his insides.

Finally, the end of the branch emerges and Oppo collapses down on the sofa, green lichen lining his lips. Rob gives him more water, thinking strangely about watering trees and plants.

Between rasps, he tries to speak, 'When I knew…couldn't stop… said I'd get what was coming…just like you all.'

Oppo still isn't breathing properly. Something else is wrong.

Rob opens up the waterproof. Underneath, Oppo is wearing only a dirtied and torn pair of tracksuit bottoms. Nothing on top save for the coat. His army tattoos are shrunken and tight, slightly more faded now than they were the last time Rob saw him. On his left hand side, around his stomach, an enormous gash opens and closes with his stymied breathing. Mud spills from the wound, dribbling down the sofa and adding to the pool. Rob can see stones and seeds in there, smaller twigs and the petals of flowers. A worm wraps itself around the edge of Oppo's broken skin, curiously raising its head.

'The hunt,' Oppo says. Rob looks up at him. Oppo's eyes are wide and mad, and he stares straight at Rob for the first time. 'Find Lucy.'

III

When he goes to visit Oppo at the university hospital, he realises he doesn't know his real name.

'You might have it down as a nickname or something, O-P-P-O,' he spells it out for them as if that would help at all. 'He was taken into surgery, but they said I shouldn't wait. It was yesterday.'

'He might be in recovery, but we don't have that name. You can go on up yourself and ask the nurse in charge, maybe describe your friend to her.'

The nurse on duty up in the recovery ward doesn't recognise the description, and Rob feels foolish trying to describe the symptoms. He feels awful even talking about Oppo as a homeless person, like that descriptor somehow denigrates him. If he'd known how much trouble the guy was in, would he have taken him in? He likes to think so, and he imagines them living together for a little while, just whilst Oppo gets back on his feet.

Instead, he's lost him.

Outside the Royal Infirmary, he crosses the road to Whitworth Park and takes a seat. He scrolls through his phone and wonders if he still has the right number, then he makes a call.

When Lucy spies him she wraps her baggy cardigan around her chest. He isn't sure why she does it, but he chooses not to attempt to hug her. She still has a streak of pink in her hair, like the old days. They sit opposite one another in The Koffee Pot and he tries to explain what happened with Oppo.

'Why did you phone me?' She doesn't show any sign of sympathy.

'Because I thought you'd want to know. It was only brief, but he was still one of us. I just feel like I should have helped.'

She sits there for a moment, not saying a word. Places her hands on the table as though she's going to leave, then doesn't.

'Fuck's sake Rob. After all that, I tried to put that day behind me.' She holds her teacup tight in both hands. 'The nightmares had actually stopped, can you believe that? I'm glad that you're okay, really I am, but coming here and bringing all of this back up, it isn't right. Alex is dead because of us, because of Oppo, he's dead. And we just left him there.'

That isn't right.

No.

Rob thinks back to the day. He remembers the four of them following the smell to the edge of the woodland. Remembers... what does he remember after that? Lucy's face, frozen in horror, Oppo bending down to inspect a torn, burnished scrap of fur. He tries to recall lighting the rook scarers. He tries to recall the four of them together in the car again, driving back. He tries, he tries, he tries.

'Rob, are you okay?'

When he looks back at her, he can feel the rawness of tears in his eyes. 'Lucy, there's bits missing. I think.'

He can almost catch the smell again. What is it?

It was a stink pit: a week old at least, maybe more. The corpses of three foxes ripped apart and shoved ignobly into the hole. It was fear she'd felt at first, but that quickly passed when she thought about the awful end that that troop must have had. Rob was explaining it to Oppo.

'The smell attracts other foxes, they come to see what the fuss is about. It's barbaric.'

'There'll be a snare nearby no doubt,' Alex said, clambering over the fallen trunk to take a look. 'Christ, what did they do to them?'

The four of them stood around the stink pit, dumbfounded. What could they do? Alex suggested giving them a proper burial, and Lucy agreed. It was Rob, or maybe it was Oppo, who said, 'Stick to the mission, light the scarers.'

There was nothing they could do now, but if they hurried, they could save some other poor creatures.

One by one they would light the bangers, making sure they weren't going to go out any time soon. It would just be a short walk back to the car, and then they'd be out of there. No confrontations, no trouble at all.

But when they got to the first rope Lucy realised Alex wasn't with them.

'He can't be far back,' Rob said, 'Let's just wait, he'll catch us up.'

She was adamant. Why, she couldn't be sure. Did she know he wouldn't catch up to them?

They found him back at the stink pit, staring into it. His body tensed up awkwardly. Chin down against his chest looking down.

'Alex?' Lucy said, holding her hand out to his shoulder.

Before she could touch him, she heard two things, almost simultaneously: the buckshot and the scream. Blood bloomed across Alex's back where the pellets had hit him, but he stayed standing. The scream hadn't come from him. Lucy turned to see Oppo, mouth rigid in a roar, leaping wildly into the woodland in the direction of the shot. How had she not seen the person who fired? She couldn't understand. The woodland wasn't so wild and thick that it could hide someone. Another shot, and the snapping of what she hoped was a branch. Then silence. Lucy ran to Alex, still standing, staring down at the stink pit.

'Alex, you need to sit down, you've been shot. It's okay, I think you're going to be alright, but you need to come with me.'

It was no good. She tried moving him, but it was as though the shot had frozen him to the ground in front of the pit.

'Rob, help me, for fuck's sake,' she said, expecting Rob to be standing there, just as confused and useless as she felt in that moment.

'But you weren't there.'

'Where was I?' Rob speaks quietly, not understanding.

'You don't remember?'

He tries to think back to that day in the woodland. The smell lodged in his nose. Oppo tightening one of the ropes that Alex had poorly knotted. But there's a haziness to it.

'I don't.' He can't even look at her. 'I didn't even know he was dead, Lucy. I didn't know.'

'I looked for you. I left Alex there to die and I looked for you.' She looks up at him, and he can see the anger inside her. 'I don't think I can forgive myself for that.'

He squeaks out a *sorry* but he knows it wouldn't do anything. How can he not remember?

Someone brings over a refill for their coffees, Lucy waves them away.

She found Rob ankle deep in the stream not far from where they'd found the stink pit. He was stood staring up at the canopy above, muttering to himself. A muffled bellow came from deep within the trees: Oppo. What or who he had found she didn't know. Lucy tried to shake Rob but, like Alex, he was rigid. Taking a deep breath she slapped him, hard, across the face, but it did nothing.

Another gunshot, echoing across the covert.

She ran back to Alex.

When she reached the stink pit though, she couldn't understand.

'He was gone, Rob, they shot him and they took him. He died, and they took him and they buried him out there on their land.' She pauses for a moment, looks him dead in the eyes, 'I put this behind me and when you called, everything came back and it was like, all the work I'd done to move on was undone.'

'I don't—' he starts to speak without really knowing what he's going to say.

'No. Please, just go.'

Rob goes to leave, but when he looks down he can see dirt under her fingernails. In the air, the rotten, sulphuric smell of the stink pit catches in his nose. Lucy's eyes are a burnished orange, her pupils a tiny slit looking at him.

'I'm going to find Oppo,' he tells her, and a part of him wonders why his words sound so much like a threat.

IV

The answer at the hospital was always just variations on a theme: no, we don't know who you're talking about, there's no-one by that name here. Finally, the nurse in charge told him he wasn't welcome there anymore, not unless he was dead or dying.

He knew some of the homeless vets, or at least, he'd seen their handwritten signs as he walked to work in the mornings. 'Ex-squaddie, just need some food.' 'Fought for queen and country, now hungry and homeless.' He was never one for any army love in, and he knew Oppo didn't have much love for them either, but maybe that's where he found his people in the end?

They used to hang out on Piccadilly Gardens, sat around the curve of concrete that set the ornate grass from the bus station. That or they'd be hanging out around the fountain. But that was before. Now, the city had clamped down on the homeless, forcing them from place to place. Brushing them under the carpet.

For a while they'd been at the Triangle, where the strange glassiness of the old Urbis stood across from the cathedral, the two of them somehow occupying both the same city and another world. That hadn't lasted either, no chance they'd be allowed to stay in such a public, tourist friendly place. So they'd been forced out again.

A shanty town of tents and placards had been set up in St Anne's square. A final stand against whoever wanted them all gone for good. They were losing their battle bit by bit. Rob remembered how it felt to lose the fight and then the spark.

There was lad sat on the steps by the Royal Exchange, a small sign next to him saying, 'Pls help, God Bless.'

'Can I get you a sandwich or a drink maybe?' he asked.

He was only twenty-five and his name was Barry. For a while he'd been living in some hotel over in Ardwick with a load of other homeless people, but that had caught fire and there was no other housing for him.

'So I'm here now.'

Rob asked about Oppo, told him the parts of the story that he could make sense of. The boy looked up at him.

'You ever meet his family?'

'They died, no brothers or sisters, nothing like that.'

'And his flat?'

'Went down this route with some friends of mine. He was one of us.'

Barry looked at him as if to say, *how stupid are you?* 'Mate, he wasn't.'

Now he's sat nursing a pint in The Castle, tucked away in the back corner of the snug, Barry's words stinging. He remembers Alex interrogating Oppo back in the car, remembers how it hurt Rob to hear him go at Oppo like that. The guy was his friend, he trusted him, and there was Alex treating him like he was trying to cross Checkpoint fucking Charlie or something. He'd been the one to persuade Alex and the others that Oppo was alright, that he was one of them. And then they'd got to the covert. And then they'd found the stink pit. And then. And then.

He calls Lucy and she picks up. For a moment, there's silence, and he wants to tell her how sorry he is, and how he wants to see her again, to listen properly.

'Please don't talk to me again,' she says.

In the background of the call, he can hear the howling of a pack of dogs, approaching hooves.

'Where are you? I think you're in—'

But she has hung up.

Lucy is all he has left from that day, and he's fucked that up. Maybe he misheard. Maybe she's fine. He thinks about Oppo, lying on his sofa in his living room, dribbling moss from between his lips, and he knows that it's a lie. He can't help her either. Fuck.

The covert had been Oppo's plan. He'd taken them there. Lured them to the stink pit. Rob doesn't know why, but he feels that it's there that he will find an answer.

V

Oppo only has three mugs so they have to share, passing the cups of tea around in a circle as though it's a playground game. Soon it becomes a bit of a laugh, Alex starts passing the mug immediately on, and eventually Lucy is left holding two. Talk is light and stupid. Topics shift like waves creeping onto a beach, and wash away as quickly. The thing they don't talk about hangs over them: the hunts, what they're all together for.

It's only when Alex says, 'So, how about we fuck up some rich cunts?' that the mood quietens down.

The walls are thin, and outside Rob can hear the tinkling of bottles being chucked in a bin, the laughter of pub talk, and the metrolink pulling in to Shudehill. The flat is freezing cold, all of them are wearing their coats. Oppo has a thing about energy bills: he can't afford them. That's what he tells them. He's apologetic about it too. 'I guess I just got used to it,' he says when Alex brings it up.

Lucy has the photos, polaroids they'd taken on previous hunts where their attempts had been unsuccessful.

'Sometimes we're good,' she tells Oppo, 'we steer the scent away from the foxes. The hunts are supposed to be using artificial scent anyway, but they mostly just let the trail lead to the real thing, we've just been extending it. It doesn't always work though.'

'There's nothing quite like the real thing,' Alex says.

'So, I might have a better idea,' Oppo goes into a shopping bag next to him and pulls out a rope with small plastic bangers attached to it. 'Ever seen one of these?'

Alex brings a tennis racquet to the pub when they next meet. Everyone takes the piss, but he fights back. 'Come on, we're undercover right? I'm committing to this way more than you guys.'

'Yeah,' Oppo says, 'But you're the only one with a racquet mate, so now we're not four people who've been playing sports together, we're three people in sports gear and a guy with a tennis racquet. Next time, if we're going to bring props, we need to agree on them beforehand. Okay?'

Since when had Oppo taken the lead for them all? Rob can't remember, but his decisions made sense. With him giving the orders they were more organised, smarter. They felt like they had a stronger purpose. Oppo had been the missing link they'd been looking for. Meeting like this, dressed up in gym clothes in the middle of a Spoons, it was a smart idea. Though it felt a bit stupid at first, being so clandestine, it was better to be on the right side of cautious than not.

Alex hides the tennis racquet under the table, and Oppo brings out an A-Z, a couple of yellow post-its stuck within its pages. He turns to one of them and points at a small patch of woodland.

'See this? It's a covert, just a few miles away from this,' he points at an historical estate to the north of it. 'That's the ancestral home of Ronald Westgate-McKnight. He's a former MP, backbencher in Thatcher's government. Retired in the early 90's, and ever since? He's been hosting hunts on his land.'

Oppo pulls out a few newspaper clippings. 'Here they are proudly showing off their kills a few weeks before the ban. It's not stopped, because they think they're better than us. They think they can get away with it, and this covert here, this little patch? That's where they'll be going in a few weeks. I've not got many contacts from the army left, I'm sure you can guess why, but a mate of mine does private security for Mr Westgate-McKnight. He's told me it's on for the twenty-fifth of next month. Has to be on that date, come rain or shine.'

Rob meets up with Oppo a week before the twenty-fifth. Just to hang out. He goes round to Oppo's flat, wearing double layers just in case. They sink a six pack of lager quicker than they expected.

'You never wanted to aim bigger?' Oppo asks, a little drunk.

'Like what?'

'You plan for ages, you go out there, and all you end up doing is saving just one or two foxes. That's it.'

Rob pauses before answering. That's not it. Oppo doesn't understand. Still doesn't quite get it. 'It's a life. I'm saving a life. The energy we put into it, if it means an animal that would be dead isn't, then it was worth it, no matter what the cost is.'

'No matter what the cost is.' Oppo nods, as though that was an answer he'd been looking for. 'Here, I've got something for you.'

He hands Rob his lighter, a green camouflage one with some weight to it.

'It's lucky, or at least, I guess it is, since I didn't die out there.'

'Cheers,' Rob says, feeling as though it undercuts the moment.

They pick up their PlayStation controllers and don't say anything more on the subject.

The night before, and Rob can't sleep. A thought gnaws at him. Alex is still suspicious of Oppo, and he knows that he'll wind up needling him in the car tomorrow. But that isn't it.

It's not the plan either. That's all been concocted with, as he expected, military precision. Oppo's man on the inside has fed them what they need to know about dates and times, so they know that there'll be no danger as long as they get there early enough. It's just about keeping their tracks covered and staying out of sight. 'Don't look like you're trying to keep your head down,' Oppo told them, 'don't try and look too normal. Those are the people that look the most suspicious.' They've even planned to go for lunch in the pub nearby after, mingling with the people they'll have fucked over that morning. Rob imagines having a pint sat a few feet away from Ronald Westgate-McKnight MP, watching him drown his sorrows after a failure of a morning out on the hunt. It really would be special.

No, it's something else tugging at the back of his mind that he can't put his finger on.

It's probably nothing. Probably nothing at all.

VI

It's been raining, the ground deep with mud that sucks at his ankles and threatens to trap him. Rob has to pull himself free using nearby braches before he is able to enter the covert.

It took longer than he thought it would to find the place. Oppo had given the driving instructions to Alex and Alex alone. Each of them had been trusted with just one part of a whole. He'd compartmentalised them and Rob hadn't even noticed it. He'd only been half paying attention once they'd come off the motorway, but once he drove past The George & Dragon for the third time, he'd got himself back on track.

He remembers few things about the geography of the place, and in the years since, the trees have been cut back, broken fences mended. But he knows he is in the right place. He didn't notice it the last time he was here, but he can tell that nothing lives in this spot. Before he set foot in the covert he could hear the sound of blackbirds in a nearby tree, a far off herd of cattle moving against their will, but all of that evaporated the moment he stepped beyond the treeline. In here, there is no birdsong. The wind doesn't whistle through the trees, though he can see the leaves moving, cautiously.

Suddenly, the sound of his own walking, breaking fallen branches underfoot, and his nervous, heavy breathing, feels like an intrusion.

Prising his foot out of another deep puddle of mud, he carries on.

He remembers the first time him, Lucy and Alex all went out together. They drove out towards the Wirral, he can't remember exactly where it was. They'd followed the hunt for a while, watching the toffs in their stupid fucking outfits whipping their horses with riding crops, chasing down the hounds.

Lucy had been the one to run in. A pack of hounds were scrummed up around another animal, rolling and barking. She just ran in there, screaming her head off. It was enough to scare the dogs off for just a moment and there, in the middle of the pack, was a small fox. Not more than a year old. She picked it up, holding it tight against her chest so it didn't bite her. The dogs didn't know what to do. Rob and Alex had stood, stupefied. Would either of them have done the same thing? Not a chance.

He can't help but feel now that bringing Oppo into everything put a full stop on a story that should have been longer. What the three of them could have done together. It's all his fault. Not Oppo's, but Rob's. Alex died back on that day but Rob feels it claw at him like a recent wound. Lucy hurts the most. If he'd said something when they met up that day. Warned her. Maybe he could have helped.

No, he thinks, no; he'd most likely be dead. Like the rest of them.

What has Oppo done?

The smell of it catches in his nose, worse than before. He trudges on towards his target. Then he catches sight of something in the trees. It's one of the rope scarers, still hanging up there, years old. How is that possible? By now the branches would have fallen in the wind, or the rope would have frayed and the bangers crashed to the ground. But there they are. This place is exactly as he remembers it, as though it were stuck in time, paused. Waiting for him.

Up ahead, the bloodied mulch of the stink pit is stark against the rest of the covert. Fox paws hang limp from the lip, a head is half buried under a mound of leaves. Rob spots a tail, still thick and bushy, peering out from between a pile of twigs.

These people, he thinks, don't want anything to belong.

This is a dead space.

He gets up close to the stink pit, covering his mouth with his sleeve. What is it that drew him here? That drew them all here in the first place? Oppo. Why did he want them to come?

The leaves bristle, and the twigs shift. From deep in the pit there is the scream of a pained animal. From underneath the leaves he can see the jaw of a fox snapping open and closed, taking desperate final breaths.

'I'm sorry,' he tries to say.

Then, another sound, the suck of mud being shifted and moved. From the centre of the pit, a hand rises up, nails broken, fingers bent and twisted into strange unnatural shapes. Rob steps back and trips on a fallen branch, crashing to the floor. He watches as the hand rises up and out of the pit, and he can see pockmarked holes in the skin where buckshot has torn through it. Alex. It clasps hold of a clump of mud and tries to pull itself further out. The mud is too slippery to get purchase, and the hand struggles, slipping back into the stink pit. It would be almost funny if it wasn't so horrifying, Rob thinks.

A rustling in the trees.

The padding of paws on the ground.

The two-tone clip clop of a horse.

He hears all of those things and he looks back at the stink pit, as though asking it for advice, for help. Without understanding, he knows that they are coming. He is on their land, in a bigger sense than he can ever understand. They own it all, and Oppo brought Alex and Rob and Lucy here for a hunt, that much is true.

The stink pit bubbles and froths, a brown foam dribbling over the side of the dead. It's expanding. Alex's hand remains jutting out at the edge, but Rob watches as the body of one of the foxes tips and falls in, subsumed by the rest of the pit.

Then he sees what it was making room for. A human head bobs on the surface. At first he thinks it belongs to Alex, but the long hair and the distinct pink streak tells him otherwise.

Run, he thinks. But that wouldn't do him any good. It didn't do Lucy any good, did it? They've been marked, for whatever reason.

There's a flash of red outside the covert.

Something bounding through the trees.

He could try. There was a time years ago when the fight was always in him, and he knows that over the years it's been drained away slowly. But that itch still lingers and he can feel it. The anger, the push.

Oppo's cigarette lighter feels heavy in his pocket and Rob pulls it out. The rope scarers still hang from the trees. This place hasn't moved in time like the rest of the world. He gets that now.

There was always the danger of burning the place down with the bangers, but fuck it, nothing's alive here and this covert can burn for a thousand years for all he cares. The first scarer is just a few feet away.

There is movement in the trees up ahead.

They are coming.

He runs.

The first scarer is easy to light, but he knows the time it will take for it to start to go off. The rope is burning thick though, and they hung it far too close to the leaves on the trees around it.

He remembers the positions of all of them; there is no way he has the time to get to them all, but he forces himself onward to the next one.

As he lights the second scarer, he looks behind him. A handful of leaves have caught. They're burning up quick, but there's the tell-tale sign of smoke coming from the floor. He hopes it's dry enough.

But then, an animal bursts from the treeline into the covert, and he can see it coming for him, and it's a hound but it's not a hound, it's something else entirely, occupying the space a hound should. It's made of ancient things: the wood of oaks that have survived for centuries, the insects that live within the bark. He doesn't understand it and he doesn't want to. These places aren't for people like him.

Instead, he runs. It gives chase.

A horn blows and within the notes that play he can hear the day in the covert replaying, buckshot being fired, and all too human, guttural screams of Lucy. He can hear his own cowardice. But he doesn't stop. He keeps on running.

The thing chasing him is right behind him now, he can feel it's breath, hot and wet against his legs. It should have caught him, killed him or dragged him down into the stink pit with the rest of them, but he's ahead of it still. It's the drive. He hasn't felt it rise up in him in years, not since the day he was last here. It pushes him, gives him a strength he forgot he ever had. He can't light the rest of the scarers, but hopefully he's done something, whatever that may be.

He'll keep running because the fight within him isn't dead and he can't imagine it ever will be.

VII

When he tries to use the toilets at Piccadilly station he gets kicked out by security.

'I'm getting a train,' he tries to say, but they just laugh at him.

'This is private property mate,' they say as they force him out of the nearest exit. 'Don't try and come back, we know your face now.'

He can see the little bodycams attached to their vests.

He cobbles together enough money to get some food, and though the benches he comes across in the city centre are odd shapes, stopping anyone out there from sleeping on them, he can at least sit down for a while and eat, watching Manchester carry on.

Running is the key, he's found. Staying hidden, always on the move.

It's time to move on when he hears the strange drumming of wooden claws on pavement, when the food he tries to eat is filled with mulch and grass, or when he hears the horrible sound of the horns that remind him of the day he's been running from. He was doing it before, he thinks, getting out of it, getting a normal job and trying to pretend he was living a normal life.

At night, he curls up in the doorways of boarded up shops. Forgotten spaces in the city. For the first week he found a derelict newsagents over in Ancoats, and was able to move some boards around to get inside. The rain came in through a few holes in the roof but it was quiet and safe.

After four nights of sleeping in there he noticed a sign on the door. Acquired for development. Some new flats. The artist's impression showed a beautiful courtyard with children and families playing, but all he could focus on were the gates at either end. He knew it was them and it was time to move on. All of his things fit into a single bag now, all the easier for him to pick up and go. Oppo taught him that once, though he wonders sometimes where that lesson even came from. He was no army man, after all.

One morning, when he finds himself walking around the city, he realises that he's taken the space that he thought Oppo was in. He remembers how that turned out, finding Oppo in his flat the way he did. He imagines sitting down right where he is on the metro tracks, letting either the tram or the hunt come for him.

Then there's a morning when he wakes up to a blinding autumn sun, and a figure standing above him.

'They're coming for you.'

It takes a him moment to recognise Barry, who holds out a hand and helps him up.

'You need to get out of the city. Go somewhere else. This place, it's all theirs now.'

Rob is just about able to say, 'where should I go?' He thinks about Liverpool or Lancaster, maybe further south, Nottingham or Birmingham. Cities where no-one knows him, where he can truly get lost.

But when he looks up Barry is gone, and the question hangs in the cold morning air.

He finds himself in Morcombe by chance. Hitchhiking his way up north, a friendly couple drop him off in the seaside town, telling him, 'This is as far as we're going.' He spends an evening sitting on the beach, watching the sun catch the edges of waves. Dogs bound around him playfully, before running back to their owners. On the water, unmanned boats bob up and down; they'll be grounded in the morning when the tide goes back out again. He is at the edge of the country and all he can see beyond is salt and sea. It means nothing, but looking out at the horizon he says a quiet, 'sorry.' It could be for

Alex, or Lucy, or even Oppo. All of them. How long has he been running now? Six months, maybe more. Scraping together coins for hostels, eating in soup kitchens and shelters. He's slept in doorways and parks, until they come and move him on. He's understood hunger and thirst like he never knew he'd understand it. When he tries to rest he can sense them coming for him, and he understands what it is to be hunted.

A dog rushes past him, and he's gripped by a sudden fear that they are here and have found him; a fear that dissipates quickly. The couple to whom the dog belongs walk past moments later, picking up a tennis ball and throwing it towards the water. How quickly, he thinks, did he resign himself to his fate. All of the running, all of the hiding was over, and that was such a relief.

He's going to stop now. This is the place he will have his last stand. Should it ever come. He has been putting all of the dead things in his life into a stink pit deep inside him, and it's done him no good. All it ends up bringing is more of the dead.

Using the last of the money he brought with him from Manchester he checks in to a run-down hostel half a mile from the beach. That night he lies on his bunk listening to the quiet sobs of a man a few beds over from him. The next day he finds some work behind a bar, cash in hand. He gives the landlord a fake name.

There is some time missing. The hound is at his feet in the covert and he's running. He's running and running and then, he's in Manchester. How did he get away from it, when it was so close? Rob can't remember.

It's a thought that plagues him when he's behind the bar on the quiet days, when the rush of customers and constant need to remember orders isn't distracting him. Sometimes he searches the internet to see if there's any news about a fire on Ronald Westgate-McKnight's land, but there's never anything. The way time moved in that space, it could still be burning now.

At night he replays the events over both days in the covert, and the things that happened after, over and over. Those pieces of missing time haunt him. He remembers the strange thing chasing him, a void in the world where a hound was missing and whatever it was instead had taken its place. Spaces in the city where people were no longer allowed to exist.

He's collecting glasses one night when he overhears a conversation. Two men sitting at a table in the snug, nursing the dregs of their pints.

'They've bought up the three derelict shops near the police station, over on Raby street.'

'The old fish and chip place?'

'Aye, a few others too. Going to tear them down and build a couple of blocks of flats I heard. They'll be selling them off with nice sea views.'

'Load of bollocks if you ask me.'

Rob walks up that way after he closes up. The fish and chip shop is shuttered up, as is another place a few yards up on the other side of the road. It's not much right now, but soon it knows it will be a building site, walls up on all sides plastered with artist's impressions of modern, beautiful buildings and gated gardens. They are here now and he knows they have come for him.

VIII

When they do come for him, he's on the beach. It's night and the tide just about covers his feet, but he doesn't mind. He sits down in the soft, damp sand, and watches the boats. Oppo sits down next to him.

'Hard man to find,' Oppo says.

'Sorry. I don't think I ever knew who you really were.'

Oppo doesn't say anything.

'You brought us all to that place. It's just me now. I think I understand.'

There's a cheer that comes from a bar near the promenade, a laddish shout from a football game. Rob looks down in front of him, and between his legs he watches as a red tail lifts from a fissure in the sand and drops. Mud bubbles up from the ground. He can smell the dead again.

'I looked at my hands this morning,' he tells Oppo, 'and I saw dirt under my fingernails. I think I've had dirt under them all this time and I just never even noticed.'

There's a horn, and it comes from the promenade. Within its sound are the events of the first day in the covert and the years after. He can hear himself running away and hiding for so long. He can hear Oppo bleeding stagnant mud in his living room and his desperate search for him in the hospital. He can hear Alex and Lucy. A pit opens up in his mind and he looks inside it and sees how he escaped those days in the covert. How he ran and ran and how they could have caught him, but the thrill of the chase was what they wanted. It's fun they've been having with them. Rob and Lucy and Alex and Oppo, and everyone else who isn't one of them. They're all just little toys to be played with. There are traps, he understands, in every place in the country. Rules made by them for them. There was no escape. There never was.

In front of him, the stink pit opens up, a mound of the dead clambering to get out. He can see Lucy and Alex in there, foxes and birds and other people too. The smell is horrible and intoxicating. It makes him sick but he cannot stop himself from smelling it.

Rob turns to look at the promenade: a harras of horses stand proudly, and mounted upon them are a group of men he cannot quite see, their beautifully maintained red uniforms stark against the nightlights of the town. At their feet, a pack of misshapen hounds, their bodies made of ancient English soil and insects and dirt, slaver and wait for their master's orders.

Oppo is no longer next to him. Perhaps he never was.

|Habitual|

~

20.

January: the walls of his flat sticky with damp, blackened spots growing on the ceiling, trailing down the walls. He moves furniture to discover mould crawling up the backs of sofas and bookshelves. Summer in the place had been bad; they'd been invaded by rats and flies – overspill from the restaurant next door that got shut down after it failed another inspection. But this is so much worse than he could have expected. People in his house threaten to move out and then do, dissolving into London: Pete and Den had bought a houseboat somewhere in the tangle of rivers and canals around Hackney, Frankie was heading back up to Sheffield to move in with her parents again. When Gawel tells him over a cuppa one night that he's found a bunch of other delivery drivers who have a spare room, and he's leaving in a week, he decides it's time for him to go too.

He dreads to think about living alone, how much the loneliness gets to him, chills him; makes him want a drink. That road should have been behind him long ago but there it is again, rearing its head, and he cannot think of that right now.

So he signs up to every site he can, trawls the ads, swipes and swipes. But the prices are high, too much for him, and every place he finds that looks like it might be good is gone, or going, or so competitive he wouldn't stand a chance.

Christ. What is this city becoming? he thinks, nursing another cup of tea with shaking hands.

19.

They send him a text, and for some reason his phone doesn't flag it as spam. He opens it unconsciously.

Your zone one property is waiting for you. Get paid to live in luxury.

A con. Clearly.

He ignores it and goes back to serving the next customer their latte.

Later, on his way home, he eyes it again. Why is it catching his eye so much? Why does he feel so drawn to it? He can't explain. The night has fallen earlier than he expected, and the lights from takeaways and passing cars dance around him on the top floor of the bus. He's not looking forward to heading home, the place will feel cold and empty with so many of them gone. Everyone feels so distant from him now, all of them moving on in ways he has never been able to: settling down, having a family, buying a home, making a life for themselves. He's never considered the thing he's made as some kind of a life. Just a series of days and weeks that have happened. No trajectory, barely any memories of some of those times.

That's the old days, though. Best not to think of those.

But he can't help it. Not when it's night and there's people a few pints deep, singing and chatting on the bus, and the warmth of it, the happiness of them, clings to him like cigarette smoke. He'll shower when he gets in. Bathe. Scrub it off.

When he opens his front door, he flicks the light switch in the hallway and… nothing. The bulb has gone. Just what he needs. He flicks his phone torch on and shines it up along the hallway. Spare bulbs are where now? Did they ever buy any? Possibly the power to the whole place has gone, which would be perfect.

Then his torch catches something in the air around the bulb, and a fragment of light cracks open, like a bird hatching. He squints up at the light fitting, shines the torch up there.

Flies. Hundreds of them, crammed around the bulb, blocking the light out.

That night he opens the message again and clicks the link.

18.

Over the road from his place, as he's hauling the last of his boxes into the back of the rental, someone lies prone on the ground, face down against the kerb. People walk past and glance down but do nothing. *Just another lost Londoner*, he thinks. Someone falling through the cracks of the city. It seems so much easier to do that now than ever before. Could have been him once upon a time, the way he'd been.

The city could have swallowed him up in that first year. Either the job would have done it for him, or the drink. Probably both.

Not now, though. New place. Incredible location. High up above everyone else.

He'll be a king.

When he'd spoken to the rep on the phone, they'd been enthusiastic. No, they didn't need to meet him face to face. No need. He was the ideal candidate. 'It's practically empty,' they told him. 'A few workmen every now and then, but no one lives there.' Every flat had been sold, but all to foreign investors. Once, one summer, the son of a dignitary from Dubai showed up for a week, but didn't come back again.

'It represents a substantial investment for our clients, so it's good to have someone in the building, keeping an eye on things.'

Like a concierge, or a security guard? he'd asked.

'Both, but you get the flat rent free, there's a gym on the fifteenth floor, and an infinity pool on the twentieth. You get access to all of it. Just keep an eye on the place.'

The keys were in a lock box, they said. They would text him the code. The man on the phone never asked him if he wanted the job or the flat, it was just assumed that the answer was yes. Of course, they were right.

A police van pulls up next to the man on the road. They check his pulse and haul him up by his arms and legs, chucking him into the back of the van with little fanfare, making jokes and laughing the whole time.

17.

The building is in Canary Wharf, strange and emptied at the weekend when he chooses to move. In the docks, enormous luxury yachts sit moored, and he wonders if the people staying in them own some of the flats in the building. There's the gentle dip of oars as a handful of kayaks row alongside them, dwarfed.

This whole place is a playground, he thinks. The rich buying up flats and houses everywhere and never living in them. Places in the city closing off more and more from people like him. When did it all turn into a theme park? He can't remember, but he knows it happened in his lifetime.

He finds the lockbox and picks up the keys before heading inside.

The lobby is enormous, seeming to stretch out further than should be possible. In front of him, a ringed leather sofa welcomes him, and above it, a luxurious glass chandelier. Mirrors everywhere reflect the opulence and extravagance, but somehow refuse to capture him. Trailing his suitcase behind him, containing his few possessions, he feels like an intruder. *Don't make too much noise, you'll wake…* but then he remembers there's no one to wake.

A screen in front of the lifts asks him which floor he'd like and he selects the eighteenth. The doors open silently to a sleek metal box. No buttons on the inside; not even, as far as he can tell, an emergency button. The doors shut and the lift starts making its way up, except that's not what it feels like. His stomach lurches, and he feels less like he is ascending than descending. Drilling down into the ground. Numbers on a small screen above the doors climb up and up, but he knows deep inside himself that it is down.

It's a surprise, then, when he opens the door into the flat, and the first thing he catches a glimpse of is the view: London, stretching itself out to the horizon. All of it distant, unreachable, but present. *Like a model village*, he thinks. The city fills the windows, draws him in. So much so that he almost doesn't take in any of the flat itself. Whoever owns the place hasn't done much to it: the big open space he's stood in has a living area with a sofa and chair facing a large flatscreen TV; to his right is a long white dining table, ten or so chairs neatly tucked in, light bulbs dangling over it and a wood burner enclosed within a glass case separating it from the kitchen. Doors on either side of the room lead, presumably, to the bedrooms, study and bathrooms.

He lets go of the suitcase and flops down on the chair, staring out of the window as a handful of boats shoot through the Thames.

He could get used to this.

16.

Daytimes he walks the corridors. Grabs the lift to the next floor, ignores the lurching feeling of the lift, always telling him he's going the wrong way, and explores every corner of the building. The rep was right. The place is totally empty. A ghost town.

On the twentieth floor, deckchairs lie unused and spread out across a wooden deck, overlooking the infinity pool. If he swims to the very edge of the water, he can look straight down: a twenty-storey drop to the street. When he clumsily attempts lengths, he can't help but feel like a disturbance.

In the gym, the dull *thunk* of a machine he's using, or the *clink* of weights knocking against each other, are intrusions in the silence.

Every noise he makes, another invasion. Every step, another message that he doesn't belong. But he shakes it off.

15.

The nights are beyond quiet. Thick glass on every wall of the flat means that, with the windows closed, no noise gets in. He can see the lights of the city dancing, cars, planes, boats and people at all times every day, and yet he hears nothing. If he wanted to, he could let it all in, but that wouldn't be right. *The building wouldn't want that*, he thinks. So he flicks the TV on and leaves it running all night, the volume low enough for the noise to be a drone, filling the gaps. He's so used to the sounds of homes filled with people, creaking floorboards, toilets flushing at odd hours, low-level chatter. The wish to drown out the silence with something lingers inside him. Used to be that the drink would help, but he won't do that. He won't ever go down that road again. The drink is why he found himself in his mid-forties still living in flat-shares, working shitty jobs for shitty pay. When he thinks about it, really tries to think, he knows it could all be traced back to school and the things that happened. No kid should have to go through that. Growing up where he did didn't help either. But he won't let it take hold of him again. He cannot. So he lets the news, reality shows and sports wash over him quietly instead.

14.

Once a week or so he heads outside for food. There's a small convenience store a few roads over which he uses for his weekly shop. Outside there is a freshness to the world, something he realises he has missed. Each time he tells himself he'll crack open a window, spend more time on the roof garden in the pool, go out for a run. But when he returns to the building, he cannot bring himself to do that.

13.

A sound wakes him. It is the middle of the night, and the blue-tinged TV screen provides light enough for him to see. A scraping. Above him? Below him? It's hard to tell. He climbs out of bed and tries to pinpoint the location of it. There: right above him. Footsteps on the ceiling, a chair being moved, the quiet murmur of conversation.

Someone else is here.

The rep said they'd text if someone was visiting. Maybe they just forgot.

He can investigate in the morning. Knock on the door of the flat immediately above him, offer a cup of tea or something. Closing his eyes, he tries to fall back to sleep.

But the noise rises. Rises. Rises.

What at first had been the low dull scraping of a chair now sounds like a long fingernail dragging itself down a rusted pipe. The footsteps on the ceiling; a cacophony of giants crushing the floorboards beneath their feet. The quiet murmur of conversation; a horrible, raucous laughter directed at him.

The sounds fill his room and he thinks it might be better in the living room. He grabs his duvet and hauls it into the open space, but even there the sound is deafening.

It's beyond his understanding. As though someone has turned an amp up to full volume and planted it in his head. How can anything be so loud?

He shuts his eyes. Squeezes them closed. Please just stop. Just stop. Please.

But nothing works.

He could call someone. Environmental services? He briefly recalls a couple of blokes showing up at the door of a house party once when he was a teenager. Trying to get them to turn the music down. Fuck lot of good that did.

Before he really understands why, he's in the hallway heading for the lift. Even out here, the noise is present. Scraping and laughing. He selects the next floor up and feels that strange lurch of the lift rising (descending).

The noise is louder now. An unbearable sound. He feels tears in his eyes and a part of him wants to reach into his sockets, push his fingers right to the back of them and tear his eyeballs out. As though that might just stop it.

Anything to make it stop.

The bell of the lift arriving at its destination is barely audible, and as the doors open, the wails and screams, the tearing and ripping, rises and rises and rises and...

Stops.

The corridor is silent. At the end, heading for the stairs, he spots a couple of police officers, one of them with a shock of ginger hair awkwardly shoved beneath his hat.

'Everything alright?' he tries to call out, but his voice is weak.

Still, one of them turns and for a moment it is as though he is seen. But they don't acknowledge him and leave through the stairwell door.

By the time he makes it there, they are long gone, and the door to the flat above him is locked.

He goes back to bed and tries, desperately, to sleep again.

12.

There was a time when the drinking was too much. Before he knew how bad it was really getting. Falling asleep on the train after work and waking up in Brighton. Making it home only to discover the bed covered in shit in the morning. Blackouts. Nights that vanished from his memory. Friends who never forgave him for things he would never recall. The more everyone retreated from him, the more he retreated from everyone else.

It was easier to be alone.

The city liked lonely people. It welcomed them in and fed them well. Like a witch in a fairy tale. That was the true secret of London; the real magic. You could blink and somehow years would pass and you'd have spent them drunk and happy. But there would be sulphur in the air. A burning lingering in the background. An oven on. A pot waiting. A hungry, hungry city waiting for its reward.

11.

A few days later he heads out again. Just to the shop on the corner. He still can't bear to go any further.

Sitting down next to it, a homeless guy with a hastily scrawled sign. *Hungry, God Bless.* Lined up next to him, a row of old *Big Issue*s. The man gives him a wave as he walks by.

'Bit of change?' he asks.

'Sorry mate, I haven't anything.'

The man looks at him briefly, eyeing him up. 'No worries,' he nods. *I see you*, the nod says, *I know what you are.*

10.

Next time he's down there he gives the man a handful of change, buys him a Coke and a sandwich from the shop too.

On the way back he glances up at the tower. There's the light in his living room that he left on.

But there is another light. A few floors up. A red light casting out into the evening sky. It reminds him of the aircraft warning lights towards the rooftop, and for a moment he thinks it might be just that. But this isn't the same kind of light. This light bathes the room it sits in.

There's another one, too. This one a few floors below. Much clearer than its counterparts, being lower to the ground. It's coming from a standing lamp next to a television. The pale yellow casts unearthly shadows around the room, making it look almost as though there are people in there.

Did the people at the agency say anything about security lights and timers? Maybe. He can't remember.

Behind him there's a commotion. He turns to see the homeless guy being hauled to his feet by two officers. The ginger hair of one of them is still vivid in his memory. Around the shop, passers-by don't even acknowledge it. Without thinking, he rushes over.

'Hey,' he shouts, 'what's going on?'

The officers ignore him. The ginger one has the homeless guy's arm bent and locked against his back, pushing him towards the back door of their van.

'Hey!'

This time they pause and turn. A few people stop, too. One of them pulls out a phone.

'What are you doing? What did he do?'

The ginger-haired one grins, deliriously happy. The other officer tips the brim of his hat.

They let go of the homeless guy, clamber back into the van and drive off.

9.

He went down the pier once, in some seaside town on the coast. Got a reading done. Thought he recognised the woman doing it, from school maybe? But he didn't like to think about those days, so he never asked. Wouldn't have mattered whether he'd asked or not anyway, he was half cut as it was. She'd shown him a picture of the Hanged Man, a rope tightly knotted around his ankle, upside down from a wooden cross, leaves brimming with life.

'Should I be worried?' he'd joked with her, and it had probably come out like *shudibworrid*, but he knew from the serene expression on the man's face that there was no need. He was trapped, but he was happy.

The rest of that day had been a blur, then a blackout. He'd woken on the train back to London. Never even remembered the name of the town. For all he knew, that whole day had been just a strange dream.

8.

It's late in the evening a few weeks later when he hears the noises. They sound as though they're coming from the living room, so he hauls himself out of bed and texts the agency, *Is anyone supposed to be coming tonight? I thought you would warn me*, but it's out of hours and they haven't responded to him before anyway, so why would they now? Creeping along the wooden floors of the room, he can hear it all getting louder and louder. Whatever it is must be on the other side of the door. *They've broken in*, he thinks, without understanding who *they* are.

The first thought he has is to apologise to the building. Touch the walls and say, *I'm sorry they're doing this to you.*

When he opens the door, the noise hits him like the first pint of the night. The room is empty but the sound is there, present in the room with him. A horrible cacophony of screaming, shouting, things breaking, ancient industrial machines burrowing and clashing. The noise is rust and broken things. It is old foundations dragging themselves out of a pit. It is the oldest noise he has ever heard and he cannot understand how he knows that. There's no point covering his ears: the noise is inside him too. It is everywhere and everything.

He stumbles to the kitchen. On the countertop there's a six-pack of Stella. None of the cans opened.

When did he buy that? He doesn't recall. But he feels that pull inside him, the desperation for a drink flooding back. He should throw them away. No, better than that, he should open every can and pour them down the sink. If their contents were still in the can, he could easily just grab one out of the bin. No, they need to be emptied completely.

But that noise.

That awful, awful noise.

He can't think. Not properly, anyway. He balls his hands into fists, pushes them against his temples, harder, harder, but it's no use. That fucking thing isn't going anywhere. Pulling the quilt from his bed, he curls up on the sofa, hoping against hope that it will just go away.

7.

What were the worst times? Not the blackout drunk nights, no. They caused anxiety, but since the memories were wiped from his brain, he had nothing to cling on to, nothing to truly feel awful about. No. There were worse. Fights. Fucks. Both with strangers. Waking up in cities he couldn't name, in flats that didn't belong to him. The constant stink. The constant need. Hands shaking all fucking day. Even after, when he'd stopped. The days he didn't drink but couldn't think of anything else. Like a constant, obsessive noise in his head. Like someone screaming at him, grabbing his hands and slapping his face with them. *Why are you drinking yourself? Why are you drinking yourself?*

6.

It doesn't stop. It will never stop.

He leaves the flat and it's there in the corridor. In the stairwell. All the way up the stairs too. No change to the volume of it. Now he can pick out individual noises: shrieks and wails, the horrible dull *shuck* of a knife going into flesh, the *crack* of a bat or a stick or something against bone. Are there drums too? Or is it the low, painful moan of someone's last few moments? Hundreds – no, thousands of voices pushing together like a wave of pain.

If he can find its source, then he can sleep, finally.

5.

He exits the stairwell and he cannot quite understand what he is looking at. The floor above his flat was identical to his, but now appears to stretch on and on beyond the building. As far as he can see, there is no endpoint to it, just corridor for what could be miles.

He stumbles towards the door of the flat directly above his. His hands are shaking, his body telling him he needs something. Just go away. Just leave and go back downstairs. Go far from here. Find somewhere new. Somewhere different. But he's turning the handle anyway. He has a horrible feeling of belonging.

Before he can open the door, it's pulled open. Two police officers barge past him, leaving the flat. They turn and smirk at him.

'They're all in there, if you're interested,' the ginger one says to him.

'Party's just getting going,' says the other in a fit of laughter.

4.

Inside, there's a smell that coats the flat. A hot, cloying smell. Something melting. Glue? It brings to mind old technology classes. The odd texture of glue against skin, the two fusing together. It's dark in the entrance, and as his eyes adjust he can make out figures. There are people here?

There's two of them in the hallway on the cusp of the living room, nursing drinks in their hands. A third sits in a chair just at the edge of his vision.

None of them move.

The world screams at him.

'Hello?' He tries to wave at them. 'Everything alright?'

As an afterthought he pathetically adds, 'I heard a noise.'

But there is no answer.

He reaches for the light switch and flicks it on.

3.

The homeless man from the shop is poised with a drink in the corridor, standing opposite a woman he doesn't recognise. They are both dead, but their bodies are solid, standing upright and posed like two dolls. The third person, in the chair, is the same, a rictus grin stapled to his face, left hand permanently forced into a thumbs up.

He walks further into the flat and there are more of them. A man in a suit caught in a freeze-frame breakdance, his bones snapped and reset at impossible angles. In the kitchen, an older woman, glamorous in a black silk dress, expensive jewellery adorning her neck and wrists, is stuck in the middle of pouring a cocktail, mouth open in a perpetual scream. Her eyes, oh Christ, her eyes. There are more still: he can see so many of them in the flat.

2.

And by the bedroom he sees it: a wooden cross and a rope. A set of steps next to it to help him. They trust him to do what he is supposed to do, what his body is telling him to do. It's about time he gave in, after all. He's just one of so many of them, slipping through the cracks of this place.

1.

He climbs up the steps and ties the rope around his ankles and he looks around the flat, at all the people cheering him on, screaming and crying and wailing, and he can feel himself being hoisted up and up and then he is upside down and he understands, he finally understands.

He opens his mouth and waits for the city to take what it needs.

|Myrmidons|

~

The bear came to Westminster at the peak of a hot summer, and did not leave until long after the seventh person was brutally murdered, their savaged corpse found strewn across the courtyard in front of Victoria station. This was before the afternoon when the tourist bus came across a bull tied to an iron stake in the road, slavering dogs circling it, growling; before the fox began stalking the streets, its skin flame red, hungry for knowledge; and before the Necromancer was put to death, burned alive in his car on Vauxhall Bridge.

We first met the Necromancer in the courtyard where the screeching hot sun burned the tarmac. He stood behind our washing, silhouetted. All three of us women who had seen him from our windows made our way out there, and each of us heard him say four words, though we each heard it in our own languages.

'This is my gift.'

The bloodied limbs he left behind were enough for each of us to collect one, and the three of us in that moment became a coven. We took the limbs and laid them on the courtyard, and we each made our wishes in the blood, smearing it across the ground and our faces. There was a warm stickiness to it that I had not expected. The limbs he brought to us were fresher than I thought they would be. Coated in blood, I thought about us all, living in this place, broken and hurt, and I felt an anger rise from the others. It was within me too, bubbling under for so long.

We set the limbs out in a shape we did not understand and had no control over, and we brought the city crashing down.

I created the bear, though it was as much my anger wrapped in bone and muscle and fur as it was a bear. Preti pulled the bull out from the marrow in the ulna of one of the limbs; it birthed screaming, spitting hot breath into the humid sky. She tethered it to the stake and wished it away. Fatima brought forth the fox, and after a time the fire that burned across its body died down and became fur.

My bear would not go far at first. It stuck close by, nuzzling against me as I made tea, groaning when I disappeared into the shower. I taught it all I knew about the world. How cold and dark and horrible it could be. The animals, our familiars, were hungry. The bear snarled and clawed at me, its pained voice asking to be fed. When it stalked down the corridor towards me, it splintered the glass in my photo frames, smashed floorboards and scarred the ceiling. I let it follow me and I trapped it, cramped and squashed in my bathroom, but the noise continued.

I bought fish from the market, cod and plaice, and passed them to him through the doorway, careful to avoid his swipes. They came back uneaten, the flesh teased, scales torn back.

There were other foods I tried, meats and vegetables, fruit and bones. Reluctantly, I caught a rat in the courtyard and brought it up. It scampered across the floor, but the bear ignored it.

'My bear is hungry,' I told the others. 'What does it eat?'

'You,' came the reply, and I felt it in my bones. *It wants you.*

I whispered to the bear the names of people I promised I would never talk of again. Stories about godawful nights when I wanted it all to end. Somewhere in the other flats, all of the women were telling stories. Preti's bull, Fatima's fox, they were satiated.

A hot stinking wave followed a snort on the other side of the door and the bull ceased crying. I carried on, spilling my blood and letting it tell my story. *Here,* it said, *this is why I am in this place, this is why I hurt. Why all of us hurt.*

And I asked it, 'Can you fix it?'

I remember crying in police stations, statements upon statements. I remember nothing.

I did not watch the bear murder the first. The second, and the rest, I saw, but not the first. Something creaked in the hallway, and I sat up in bed and saw the matted fur of the bear creeping its way out of the flat. It would return. Sleep beckoned, and I dreamt of my bear stalking the streets. I dreamt it found the one who had caused me so much pain. I dreamt that my bear tore into him.

When I awoke, my bear was panting at the foot of my bed, blood smeared and dripping from its maw. I christened it Rakshasa that night and I knew it would keep me safe.

The bull had no name.

Preti kept it staked to the ground, bound by magics only she understood. It was hungry and panicked, and we would see it sometimes, in the road, charging at traffic, desperate to feed. Preti would not allow this, and kept her stories hidden inside, the bull getting more desperate and more angry as the days passed. I worried it would break the chains that bound it to the stake, that it would release itself from its prison, but it remained stuck there in the centre of the road, cars swerving to avoid it.

Fatima's fox snuck out at night on her word. It talked to the other animals of the dark, the urban foxes, the rats and mice on the tube, and the cats. When it returned, it was satiated, belly full of knowledge. They sat together, Fatima and the fox, on the lino floor of her flat, as it vomited up the secrets it had discovered. She took a needle and carved sigils within the guts of London's darkness and we shared everything.

The Necromancer returned a few days later.

I saw him from my window as he arrived in the courtyard and left almost as quick, leaving behind a small bag.

Preti and Fatima were gone so I made my way down on my own and I opened the bag.

The dead know secrets. Things we couldn't dream of knowing. That morning, the Necromancer brought us all secrets and I took them for myself, squirrelled them away inside my flat, feeding them to the bear to keep them safe. I watched the bear crunch down on the tiny finger bones that the Necromancer had put in the bag, felt the snap of them, saw bone dust float gracefully to the floor.

Later that evening, as the bear slept, and I sat on my settee and watched its great chest heave up and down, and listened to its breath,

I whispered to it another name. This name held a different kind of power to the first, a deeper, stranger power. As though the name came not from within me, but from another source. As though I was just a vessel.

The bear's eyes shot awake and I took its fur in my fists and climbed on top of it, and rode it into the night.

I bathed in blood in the shadow of Vauxhall Bridge.

There were plans to leave, of course there were. Hundreds of them. I will do it, I will do it today, I will do it this week, this month, soon. One day.

The other two ask me about my night. I have already whispered new names to my bear and we will ride again and kill for him. I don't tell them anything but they know. We are connected in strange ways.

Fatima has made tea, and the steam from the pot rises and hangs in the air around us. They are quiet, Preti and Fatima, and I know they are communicating with each other, though they do not address me. I am being closed out.

Then, they let me in.

'He gave us a bag,' Preti says.

'And you took it for yourself,' Fatima adds, though they sound as though they are speaking as one.

I am, for the first time since the Necromancer appeared, separated from them, speaking with my own voice. It sounds lonely.

'I had to.' It's the only argument I have.

'No,' they say together, 'you wanted to.'

Rakshasa stirs in his sleep, each breath of his spilling out into the room, fogging up Fatima's windows.

I ride the bear through the streets of the city, gripping tight onto its fur. He treads his paws along Whitehall, and roars at the Thames on Vauxhall Bridge. There is a storm coming in, I can feel it rising, taste the changes in pressure. I whisper a name to the bear and off we ride, south of the river. There will be more blood tonight.

I wake to find the faint outlines of Fatima and Preti standing above me in the darkness. Behind them, the bull stands, growling like a dog, and on top of him sits the fox. Rakshasa sleeps at the foot of my bed, though he takes up most of the room in it.

'Why do you do this?' they say, and I cannot answer. It is not that I do not know, because I do know. In the darkness I hear Rakshasa chewing on the bones of tonight's dead. The bones will feed our hunger.

'Why do you do this alone?' they ask.

'I have always been alone,' I reply, though I am no longer alone. I have the bear. I need no others.

'We are more powerful together.'

'I do not care.'

When I truly manage to focus on the objects in the room, adjusting to the dark, the four of them are gone, though I can smell the bull.

Three days later the Necromancer returns to me with his bag of bones. I no longer need the bones he brings me. Rakshasa and I have our own, unending supply. I meet him in the courtyard and Rakshasa bows down on her two front legs, a reverent steam rising from her nostrils.

'There are stories,' he says, 'about a woman who rides across the city on the back of a bloodied bear.' He seems to regret his decision, and hesitates with the bag, holding it away from me.

'You gave me Rakshasa, and you brought me the bones.'

'The others have not done nearly as much as you. You are wounding this city. When I consult the maps there are streaks of blood, your tracks, all over it. Had I known you were so angry, so full of hatred...'

'You would have given me this power anyway. Preti wishes to contain it, Fatima is only interested in knowledge. The blood is necessary.' I see through him. He never cared about the others. The bull and the fox are unimportant. Preti and Fatima are tiny and insignificant. Rakshasa and I can do something. We can cleanse this city. The list of those to whom I wish to cause harm is long, and once that list is extinguished there will be more, always more.

The Necromancer leaves the bones with me, and I feel a pang of fear from him. I find his name on my list suddenly, in a moment of anger.

I kill the fox first. Rakshasa and I bound over garden fences somewhere south of Peckham, following the stink of understanding that the fox leaves behind like piss. We corner it in the backyard of a terrace house and Rakshasa devours it completely. The fox does not put up a fight, and we do not celebrate its death. Instead, I bathe in the newfound knowledge that it gives me, and I feel the power that the Necromancer bestowed on Fatima loosen and drift free from her.

When I finally leave it is in the dead of night. Before I go, I stop in our kitchen and I consider taking a knife to his throat. I do not do it that night, but I take the promise of it and I add it to my anger. As the bus pulls up I imagine him waking up to find me gone.

We are cautious when we approach the bull. It is staked to the ground in the middle of the road, where Preti keeps it. Rakshasa is cowardly in front of it, reverent even. The bear pauses and sniffs the air a few blocks away. We can sense its power, though it is lesser than ours.

'Hello Bull,' I say, approaching it. I keep my pace slow, my feet tensed, ready to turn heel and run. Rakshasa snarls and gears up to tear into the bull but I hold my hand up.

'This is mine.'

I use a kitchen knife, of course.

Do not shower. Do not wash the blood off. Let my skin be stained red. There are things they don't tell you about the blood of foxes: that it is thick with wisdom, that it smells so sweet, that it is tar-like and black. The blood of a bull is different. That blood is red with anger and frustration, that blood tastes bitter and salty. Where they mingle, amongst the hairs on my body, in the wrinkles on my wet skin, they become muddied and different. I take my finger and I run it down my skin, and I taste it, let it linger on my tongue.

The others will come. They will bring their anger. They will tell me that the coven was strong, that together we were powerful but I know that this is a lie, for I know how strong I am on my own. I have no need of them and I have no more need of the Necromancer.

I open the tiny window in the flat and I let the fresh air of the city in. I taste it on my tongue. It tastes of people sleeping, waiting to be bled. It tastes of the flames that await the Necromancer, of the spark that will ignite him later tonight. Of the bones of his that Rakshasa will feed on, and grow stronger. Of blood and sweat and fire and everything that cities are made from.

|All Honours That Are Due|

~

Donna votes for the first time in her life on a cold May morning and imagines the queue would be longer than it is. When she shows up at the school nearest to her, polling card in hand, she walks right in. There are a handful of people pottering about – rearranging cards in boxes, making cups of tea – and there are a few others standing in the wooden booths, scratching their own votes. She gives her name to the clerk, and takes a slip from him. He smiles at her, as though he knows it's her first time. When she heads into the booth she realises she's taken one next to the only unoccupied stall. She can see a pair of legs stood next to her. It reminds her of something her father once told her about urinals and she stifles a laugh.

She takes the pencil, and she's about to mark a cross against the name of a neighbour, a friend of her mum's, when she hears the man in the booth next to her whisper.

'She'll come collect. Any day now.'

The walls of the booth are a thin barrier and so, for a moment, the voice sounds as though it's coming from right behind her. Someone leaning right in and whispering in her ear. A harsh whisper that picks at the hairs and hurts the drum.

There's men who she sees on the high street every day talking to themselves. Bunch of mentals. Some of them come into the pub when she works on Fridays and sit in the corner, muttering. One of them – she's nicknamed him Yellowfingers because of his smoker's hands – she always sees arguing with no-one.

She scratches a cross on her slip and before she leaves, she sneaks a glimpse of the man in the booth next to her. He's got his back to her. Arms by his sides, staring dead ahead. A long, brown trench coat covers his body, and straggly greased hair sticks to the collar. What was it that Joanna says about men in trenchcoats?

They could have anything under there, or nothing. When she looks at Yellowfingers she spies a hump on his back, a misshaped mass between his shoulder blades. Or at least, that's what she thinks she sees the first time because as she passes him, he drops something to the floor, a small black button. Must have fallen from his coat. When she looks back up, before the booth is out of her view, the lump is gone.

At home, her mother has already gone out for the day, leaving Flora alone. There's a note on the table in the living room: she's gone down to the shops. Of course she has. Donna can see her mother sat plugging money in to the fruit machine in The Alms. She'll come home when she's lost it all and she'll say the same thing she always says. *Next time love, I was so close.* There's talk of a betting shop opening up on the high street where the florists used to be. It frightens Donna to think what would happen if that damned place was to open.

Flora is tottering about in the living room. She runs over to Donna when she sees her, dragging along the floor a small rust-coloured bear.

'Mummy!' She grabs Donna's leg and holds it tight. Donna bends down and kisses her.

'Hey you, how long have you been all alone? Where did Granny head off to?'

'Out.'

Donna stands up and looks around the living room. On the table next to the window, the ashtray sits with a small plume of smoke rising. Not long then. Thank god. She stubs the cigarette out and flicks the TV on.

In the kitchen she boils a kettle and double checks her shifts for the week. She's in tonight, but not until eight, when Flora will be fast asleep. She hopes she's already told her mother about this, and starts rehearsing the conversation if she hasn't.

But I have to work.

Well you should get a bloody job that lets you raise a daughter properly

If I could work anywhere else, don't you think I would?

You like it there

Well I wonder who I take after?

And no doubt, an hour or so into her shift, she'll look up from the bar at The Alms to see her mother totter in, dragging on the end of a cigarette. They'll make eye contact and her mother will say, 'S'fine. She's asleep,' and even in the bar, even at the distance they're stood from each other, she'll be able to smell rank, bitter cider on her breath. And no doubt, maybe an hour or so before she rings the last orders bell, her mother will stagger up to the bar demanding a drink on the house; god, if she tries to get Donna's attention by ringing the bell again. And no doubt, by the end of the night, Steve will ask her to take her sleeping mother home. All night too she'll be worried about Flora, and the first thing she'll do when she gets in is check in on her. She'll be sleeping sound as always and Donna will watch her, peaceful in bed, and think to herself that she'd have to do something really terrible to mess her up.

There's a knock at the door and she heads to answer it, expecting it to be her mother. She takes her time getting to the door, just to make her stew a bit. When she opens it though, there's no-one there. Kids. If Flora ever turned out like some of them from down the road, there'd be words.

She puts Flora to bed, and reads her a story about an elephant who loses his hat. It's a kid's book, but for some reason a tension rises in her. The elephant wanders around the jungle, pushing deeper and deeper into the undergrowth, desperately asking the animals if they've seen it. His hat is nowhere. For him, it's the most precious object he owns. For him, it is the world. The monkeys haven't seen it. The toucan just flies away shrugging. Depressed, he returns home, only to find his hat under his pillow where it has always been. Donna's palms sweat. Surely he'd know it was there. Surely he would have checked. In the back of her mind, she pictures a creature in the jungle, the kind which no-one has ever seen before, gently unlatching the door of the elephant's home, sneaking in and taking the hat, before replacing it later in the day. The kind of creature who takes joy in watching him run around panicked. *What kind of monster would do that?* she thinks. Flora giggles the whole way through, and asks her to read it again when she's finished. By the time Donna gets to the end of the second read through, Flora is fast asleep, arms splayed up.

The Alms looks welcoming on such a cold night, the warm glow of the lights pouring from the windows and inviting in passers-by. Drinkers and smokers spill out onto the streets. Inside, the talk is loud and excitable. Old regulars crowd around their usual spots, whilst throngs of teenagers, most too young to drink in there – but who really cares – shout and sing, and sometimes dance. In the corner of the room, in a leather chair she swears she's never seen before, an old woman wearing a cheap tin crown sits sipping a brandy. They make eye contact, briefly, and a terrible ache hits Donna. But it quickly passes, and she pushes her way through to the side entrance of the bar. Steve is on his own back there, the vein on his head visible. The bar is five deep, at least. He gives her a look, a mixture of *I understand* sympathy and *don't keep doing this* annoyance, and she gets right to serving. When she looks back over at the spot where she was sitting, the woman has already finished her drink and left, and the chair has been taken somewhere else.

As she's getting some pimply fifteen-year-old two cider and blacks, she notices her mother crawling in through the door, nose red flushed and arms reaching out for something to hold up.

As soon as her mother enters The Alms, Donna knows something is wrong. Her mother pushes through the crowd with a force that Donna has not seen before. Her heart catches, lodges itself somewhere high up.

She thinks one word: Flora.

Her mother is crying, and she tries to hug Donna and say something to her, but Donna isn't listening, although she catches the dreaded word, and another: *gone*. She rushes home, doesn't even tell Steve where she's heading, just runs out of The Alms and up the road to the house.

The place is as she left it. Her mother's cigarette stubbed out in the ashtray. Sofa cushions haphazardly strewn around the living room. Flora's toys exploring the carpet and surrounding floorboards. The TV on standby. Donna takes the stairs two at a time, and flings the door to Flora's bedroom open. She is gone. The bed is made, the window closed. The pillow creased in the spot she occupied not an even an hour ago.

Donna looks under the bed, she yells out Flora's name. She explores the rest of the house. Tries to make things sound playful. 'Come on out of your hidey-hole.' Looks under the kitchen table, in the cupboards. Even checks the one under the stairs that she knows Flora's scared of. But there is no Flora. She is not hiding.

Donna's mother finally makes it back to the house, and Donna launches into her as soon as she sets foot in the hallway. She says things she means but doesn't mean. For once, her mother just stands there and takes it. When Donna slaps her across the face, she barely flinches.

'What happened?' She wants to slap her again, but she holds it back. 'What happened?'

'Honestly, I just shut my eyes for one minute, I don't know what happened. I don't know.'

'Was the door open?' Her mother doesn't answer, so she grabs her by the shoulders and shakes her, shouting, 'Was the door open?'

'I don't remember.'

The police have questions. Most begin with why, and the ones that don't, she can tell are thinly veiled whys in disguise. *Why weren't you in the house when your daughter was taken? Why did you leave her alone? Why aren't you a better mother? Why did you do this to your daughter? Why did you let her be taken?*

The sergeant sips from the cup of tea she made for him, half spilled from her shaking. He asks her if she knows of anyone who might want to hurt her. She doesn't, but when she looks over at her mother, she's on the verge of tears again, gripping the arm of the chair she's sat in.

Donna takes the sergeant, whose name is Harris, up the stairs, but she can't bring herself to go into Flora's bedroom. To see that empty bed again, and the little crease in the pillow, it would be too much for her. Harris opens the door and enters the room. If he walks around Donna cannot tell, as he makes no sound. For all she knows, he's just stood there in the middle of the bedroom. When he exits, he asks her, 'Is she the kind of girl who would be likely to run away?' and Donna realises she hasn't even told him Flora's age.

When he finally finishes asking her questions, he gets up to leave. Donna is too tired to show him out, so she leaves it up to her mother to do so. Lying on the sofa she can see her mother in deep conversation with him, before opening the door and letting him out.

It is three days later when it fully hits, when Donna wakes up on the sofa in her clothes. Heading to the kitchen to pour a glass of water, she spots herself in the mirror. The shirt she's wearing, it's the same one she wore to The Alms the night Flora vanished. She hasn't washed or changed since then. The shower is up next to Flora's room, a place she has not ventured since that night. Determined to tidy herself, to get out and start searching, she places a foot on the first step. But then she looks up, and there's Flora's door, shut. Donna spends the third day on that step, weeping.

Her mother has been affected differently. There haven't been any late, drunken nights. She's even been cooking meals for Donna, every evening. Sitting next to her on the sofa and stroking her hair until her daughter drifts off, even if it's only momentary. It's as though she's been on hold for her entire life and suddenly something has been lifted from her; suddenly she is allowed to care for Donna, to look after herself. *Where has that come from?* Donna wonders, but the thought is brief.

She doesn't take part in the police search, though she wants to. Regulars from the pub stand side by side with police in a nearby field that leads to the forest. Steve links arms with Harris. Donna can see them from the window in her bedroom, spread out in a long line. They begin walking, a funereal pace across the grass, faces down. She knows what they're looking for. It doesn't bear thinking about, but it's all she can do. The line of police officers and people from the town spreads across the grassy patch towards the woods; Donna catches the flash of a press photographer, she should be there, she should be helping. If she isn't there, then what do the press think? What does everyone think? *She doesn't care. She did it.* Before she really even knows what she's doing, she's thrown her dressing gown on, shoved her slippers on the wrong feet and she's out of the door and running down the road. *I'm here to help,* she'll say. *I love my daughter and I want her back,* she'll tell them, as though it's her that needs convincing, and not them.

The press photographer is at the back of the line of searchers, getting a wide shot, when Donna sets foot on the field. A few reporters stand idling at the sidelines and when they see her, they pick up their pads and dictaphones, and make their way over to her. *How are you feeling?* one of them asks, and she has to stifle a laugh. *How am I supposed to be feeling?* she wants to say. *Have they found anything?* another reporter asks. But she doesn't say anything to them. She carries on through the field, following the flattened grass and bootprints of the search party. They are up ahead, nearing the entrance to the woods, those with linked arms parting ways to fit between the thick trees which block their way. Donna picks up the pace and starts running. Her foot catches on a loose stone and she trips, falling to the floor. People begin to turn, one by one they look behind at her, their faces offering pity, sadness, and confusion.

It's Yellowfingers who approaches her. He breaks up the line and runs over.

'Are you okay? What are you doing out here? You should be at home.' He squats to speak to her. She can feel the warmth of cameras infect her cheeks.

When she looks up, she can see them, all of them, looking back at her, burning into her. She feels as though all of her is on show. As though her clothes have melted from her and her skin and bone have dissolved and they can see right into her, at her heart and her stomach, and her mind. That they can see she has eaten this morning, and want to know why she's eating when her daughter is missing. They can see her heart is still beating and they want to know how that can be. That her mind has wandered and she hasn't thought about Flora for the last ten minutes, and how can that possibly be the mind of someone who cares? Cared.

'Let's get you home,' Yellowfingers says, holding out his hand.

The door is wide open, and the cold from outside has infected the house. She feels a chill as she's led in, and Yellowfingers finds a blanket for her. He hands her a glass of water, which she refuses, but starts drinking as soon as it's handed to her. He smells of tobacco, and when he speaks there's a familiar nerve in her that pinches when she catches the stink of booze. She thanks him, and he smiles.

'Thank you,' he replies. She doesn't know what for.

His name is Peter, ('like the Gospel,' though Donna thinks he must have said Disciple), and she can't believe she didn't know that. He's always just been Yellowfingers to her. A stupid nickname. He worked at the factory till they laid them all off.

'Overnight it was. No build up or nothing, no big announcement. One day we got up like usual, and got to the gates and they was locked. That was that. No more work there, no more work anywhere. I get help now, but it was tough, and it's costing me.' He looks over his shoulder, and Donna notices that misshaped lump on his back; the poor man.

She understands. There was a time she didn't have a job either, when she had to ask for handouts, and she knows full well the hoops they make you jump through. That kind of thing would cost anyone their sanity, but at least it's help. He's right about that.

'Sorry,' she says, 'I never offered you anything. Did you want a drink, or a bite to eat maybe?'

'Me? No, I'm alright. You don't need to offer me anything. You've done this town a world of good you have. No need to be offering anyone anything.'

He places a jaundiced hand on her shoulder and sings softly,

'Unto your youthful Queen now give.
All honours that are due
And we are sure she'll in return
Her favours shower on you.'

It's a song she remembers from her childhood, one she used to sing with gusto and verve, but today the words chill her.

She wakes up and it could be hours later. The streetlamps buzz through the gaps in her curtains. A part of her expects Yellowfingers to still be there. Not Yellowfingers. *Peter.* He isn't though. She's lost all track of time, and she should feel rested. It's the first proper sleep she's had in days but it doesn't feel good. Every part of her aches when she stands.

She approaches the stairs, intending to shower, but instead she spends the night in the corridor downstairs beneath a photo of Flora. Her mother is nowhere to be seen.

Sergeant Harris has more questions. They have searched and found nothing. They have no leads. They have no evidence. They have no idea where Flora is. He asks about Flora's father. He asks about him a lot. Where does he live? What kind of a relationship does he have with Flora? What kind of a husband was he? Donna tells Sergeant Harris that he wasn't ever her husband, and Sergeant Harris raises his eyebrow and writes something down as though it's the fucking bloodstained dagger in the drawing room. Sergeant Harris tells her that everyone in the town is out there searching. There's a social media campaign. 'Lots of tweets,' he says. 'Lots of tweets.' Tomorrow, there's going to be a press conference and if she feels up to it, she could say a few words. 'I know it's bad form, but a statement from a mother in your... state... well, that's going to inspire the public more.'

He doesn't say grieving.

He doesn't say grieving.

He doesn't say grieving.

When Sergeant Harris gets up to leave, Donna opens the door for him and on the other side of the road she spots Yellowfingers. The lump on his back is gone, and standing next to him, as though in its place, is the woman from The Alms. The tin crown on her head is even more battered and dull under the streetlamp. That woman, Donna thinks, who is she? She's never seen her before, and she's old. Her face is hidden in the shadow of the crown, but even with that on her, Donna can see the final wisps of silvery hair, can see the deep wrinkles in her face. Then there's that feeling again. That awful lost feeling she got when she first saw her sat there in the pub. She almost didn't notice it this time, because it's how she's felt since Flora went missing, but just looking at that woman, just catching her eyes for a moment, it's as though that feeling is trebled. Donna isn't sure that's possible.

Both of them are just stood there watching her. No. No it isn't her they're watching. It's the upstairs window. It's Flora's bedroom. When they catch her watching they move on quickly, but Yellowfingers smiles (pained) and gives a sympathetic wave.

As they part ways and carry on down the street, Yellowfingers (Peter) looks back at her house, up at the bedroom window, and gives a nod.

She lies in bed, and she's supposed to be sleeping but she can't. The blueish flicker of the television lights up the room. The news is on, though she's got the sound completely off. Every few minutes another photo of Flora pops up in the foreground whilst behind it footage plays of the party searching the field, and then of Donna running towards them. This sequence replays so often Donna has to check the clock to make sure time is still moving forward. It becomes hypnotic; she learns to count the two minutes and twenty seconds between Flora. There's a brief update on the weather (rain is coming), then something about a crisis overseas, and then they bring her back to Donna. She shuts her eyes. One two three four… sixty-three sixty-four sixty-five… one hundred and twenty-one… one hundred and forty, and she opens them and there she is again. A smiling picture of her daughter.

Just as quickly as it appears it vanishes again and she shuts her eyes to count. Then she hears it. Soft but anguished. It's Flora's voice coming from downstairs. She's crying. Weeping. It can't be her, but it is. Donna knows that cry anywhere. She's heard it so many times. How is she back? It doesn't matter. All that matters is that she's there.

Donna runs out of the room and follows the cries. They get louder as she approaches the landing, and she flicks the light on. The noise is coming from downstairs. Maybe the kitchen? It sounds as though she's about as far away in the house as she can be, but she's here, inside the house.

She sets foot on the stairs and the cries become deafening.

'Flora, Flora it's your mummy, it's your mummy. Everything is going to be okay, you're safe home now.'

She'll ring the police and they'll come and everything will be fine again. God, she'll keep Flora close to her for the rest of her life. She'll never let her go.

Donna gets to the foot of the stairs and Flora isn't in the living room. The television down there is on. The news is playing, silent. A picture of Flora watches her cross the room to the kitchen. That's where it is. That's where it has to be. She's on the other side of the door, crying and alone.

But when Donna opens the door, there's nothing, and the crying stops.

She goes to sleep again on the sofa, leaving the broken doors of cupboards, and the strewn remnants of whatever was in them, sprawled across the floor. In her dreams, Yellowfingers stands outside her door silently knocking.

The sound of footsteps outside her door wakes her. A child running away, playfully, little steel heels clacking along the pathway. She hauls herself up from the sofa and makes her way to the door. It's almost dreamlike, she feels. Light and soft. Her feet don't connect with the floor. For a second she doesn't even recognise the house she's in. It's dark and claustrophobic.

When she opens the door, there is no-one to be seen. Whoever ran up, they were quick to get away, or she was slow to walk; she isn't sure. Instead, what lies in front of her is a brilliant display of colour, and a rising smell of sweetness that combats the stink of the lukewarm food that lies where she threw it the night before, in a pool of slowly curdling milk. There are bunches of flowers, laid out on the doorstep, their yellow petals reaching out towards her like uncurled fingers. Beyond the doorstep there are more flowers, the path is covered in them, bunches wrapped in ribbon, bouquets in cloths, single stems strewn all around. Every anther pointing right towards her door, towards her. She feels them, staring at her. The way that woman stared at her.

She retreats inside, slams the door and hooks the chain on it.

Knocking wakes her again, and she almost doesn't even bother getting up to answer. The thought of opening it to no-one, to more of those flowers, it's too much. But then she hears her mother's voice through the letterbox.

'Are you there Donna? The door's locked, can you let me in?'

Donna forces herself up, off the sofa and she opens the door. Her mother comes in, trying to keep a solemn face, to look mournful, but the corners of a smile are there, and her rosy cheeks betray her even more.

The two of them, mother and daughter, sit together on the sofa with a cup of tea. It's too hot for Donna, but her mother – asbestos mouth and all – takes a long sip.

'I spoke with the head of the investigation, and he says they're doing all they can to find your daughter.'

'Flora.'

'What's that dear?'

'Her name, it's Flora. She's your granddaughter.' There is something inside Donna which she hasn't felt before, something rising, so much she wants to say to her mother, but really, just one question will do. 'Where have you been?'

'I just popped to the shops to get some essentials.'

'Not just today, but yesterday, and the day before, where were you? I was scared. I was all alone here. I thought I heard her, I thought I was going mad, and you weren't here.'

Her mother puts her mug down on the floor and puts her arm around Donna, whispers in her ear, tells her that everything is going to be alright. That no matter what happens they'll find a way through it all.

'How can you be so sure?' Donna says between tears. 'She's gone, and I don't know if she's going to come back.'

'Hush now, things are going be better now, so much better. I don't know where she is, but I have dreamed about her every single night since she has been gone. She comes to me, or I go to her. I can never tell. We don't speak, and she has a garland of beautiful yellow flowers. She looks at me as though to say thank you. Don't you see, I dream that she is happy where she is.'

'I heard her,' Donna says. 'She was in this house. She was right here and I heard her.'

'We lost a dog once. Do you remember?'

'This isn't like losing a dog.'

'But you don't remember do you?'

Donna shakes her head. No.

'We were down in the park, it was early January and you ran on ahead, bouncing down on the crisp grass. You loved the noise it made. You must have only been four years old at the time. We had a dog then, you called him Shovel, because of how much he liked to dig up the garden.'

'Shovel? I don't remember.'

'You had Shovel on the lead, but he was dragging you further and further away from us. It was the park though, so we weren't worried or anything. I found you a bit further up the path. You still had the lead in your hand, though it had split. We asked you where Shovel was. What happened to him. And do you remember what you said?'

'The Queen took him.' Donna says it without thinking, without even knowing what she means.

'That's right. That's what you told us. And I told you something that day, all those years ago.'

'The good will come.' A phrase that sits within her, but one she has no memory of hearing.

'And it did. The frost passed, and the sun and rain came. We had a good year, a happy year. Perhaps we will have another good year now.'

And she sings Donna a song from her childhood:

'Unto your youthful Queen now give.
All honours that are due
And we are sure she'll in return
Her favours shower on you.'

And it's the same song that Yellowfingers sang to her when he was in her home. It's just a song that everyone in the village sings though. A song for the good harvest, for ripe and plentiful crops, for good luck in the coming years. Donna remembers singing it back in school, on festival days. It's a song asking for good fortune in the future and Donna can feel it under her skin, the melody pricking her veins and infecting her blood, rushing around her body, warming it, bringing the colour back. She feels clean, though she hasn't washed in days. It's as though her entire body has been ossified for weeks, marbled and stony, and only now is it waking up and loosening. Her blood, once iced, is melting. Her head feels clearer.

'Come here now,' her mother says. 'It's going to be alright now. Everything is going to be so much better now.'

She lies down on her mother's lap, the way she did when she was younger, and looks up at the ceiling. Her ear is next to her mother's body and she can hear her heart beat, and they are in sync.

She looks across at the rug in front of the television, the space where Flora used to play. There she is, in Donna's mind, piling bricks, sitting her dolls up at the tiny plastic table, muttering to herself. What did she sound like? A terror grips Donna when she tries to remember her daughter's voice. She cannot recall it.

'I can't remember her voice,' she says to her mother, who nods expectedly.

'Everything is going to be so much better now,' she repeats, stroking her daughter's hair the way she did once before, and Donna can remember it so vividly now, the touch of her mother against her scalp when she was younger.

Why can't she hear her daughter's voice?

She catches a glint of sunlight from between the curtains, brighter than she thinks the sun has ever been before. It beams in and almost blinds her, but when her eyes adjust, all that remains in the periphery of her vision are little sunspots, a memory coloured yellow.

|A Visitor's Guide to Penge Magic|
|(Annotated)|

~

'You can walk around in New York while you sleep in Penge'
— David Bowie

The important things first: my name is Robert Harrison and I have found the William Hone book. Those of you lurking on the horror forums and the groups on Facebook have long given up on ever finding it, though I dare say that many people were never really that bothered in the first place. Why would anyone care about the folklore of a place like Penge?

I have to admit that for a while I felt the exact same way. What has this place got that other places don't? It's a terminus for those who haven't the means to live in London but oh so want to pretend they're still a part of the city. The edgelands between London and Kent. It's nowhere.

It's not real. That's what I thought when I found it, hidden on a shelf of tattered old books in a shop in Sydenham. A tiny blue volume. *Hone* labelled gold on the side, and beneath that on the spine: *A Visitors Guide to Penge Magic*. Of course the owner of the shop had no idea where the book had come from. A second-hand donation. The purchase of a job lot from someone's home. The remains of a local library. It could have been any of those, he admitted. No doubt this was the real thing. Dated 1880 on the inside cover. The pages were off-colour but otherwise of a good condition. On the cover itself there were perhaps a few scuff marks on the front, and yet on the back, a large black mark running up the centre, as though someone had taken a candle and very deliberately applied it to the book. An odd thing to do, which seemed to have done nothing except ruin an overall decent edition. What a waste.

The entries in the book mostly detail Hone's social life from his time in the area, friendships, dining, entertainment. He thought he was Pepys. But every now and again there are entries which do not belong. Stories of magic. Unexplained phenomena. Mostly garnered, it seems, from his nights drinking in the Crooked Billet, and about as trustworthy as stories told by inebriates are likely to be. However, the edition I discovered contains a second voice. An annotator. Name unknown, with rather scruffy writing. He has commented on each of these odd stories, though I must admit that he seems to have taken them far more seriously than I have.

Perhaps the easiest thing to do would be to present these stranger entries to you, along with their annotations from the second, unknown individual, and my own notes on their veracity. You will, I'm sure, come to understand a number of things. Firstly, Hone was a drunk and a liar, relying entirely on the stories of barflies, vagabonds (and very likely criminals) to describe the area. The second is that our unnamed narrator is clearly unstable. He shows signs of delusion, which get markedly worse as the book progresses. If he still lives, I worry about his overall mental state.

> *'Do not travel south of the river my dear*
> *It's safer here in the north*
> *Do not travel south of the river my dear*
> *You'll wish you had never been born.'*
> *Anon, 1815*

Mum read this poem to me when I was a child. Said it was an old family poem. Used to help me get to sleep at night. I still say it to myself now. Why is it here?

It's safe to say Anon doesn't exist and this is Hone writing. How do we know? Firstly, the poem is terrible. 1815 is most likely just a date plucked from the ether for the purposes of this text. Maybe our anonymous annotator is telling the truth here, and perhaps what we have here is a book passed down through the family. My own mother used to read Grimms' fairy tales without attribution, and it's very likely that someone could grow up thinking that these stories and poems were just a part of family tradition.

Hag-Stones

In the back room of the Crooked Billet, an old woman, her thirst long quenched (but who was still drinking) presented me with a hag-stone, which, if I held it to my ear, produced the faint sounds of a distant town. I could hear the bustling of people, and the ferocious wheels of carriages on cobblestones. The stone itself was unremarkable except that the hole that ran through its centre appeared man-made, and not the product of erosion. More curious, on the edge of the stone, there was an initial (or so it appears) etched in. An 'R'. The craftsmanship was not particularly impressive, though the trick it produced was mildly amusing.

My stone! I carved the R into it yesterday. Must have read this passage already. Need to get some sleep.

Well, this is rather straightforward isn't it? Our annotator read the passage perhaps a week or so earlier, and copied the work; forgot he'd read the damned thing and upon reading it again, well, you get the idea.

As for the description of the sounds that Hone heard when he placed the hag-stone to his ear? Who knows, but trickery knows no bounds. Hone appears willing to believe a great many things and even he only dedicates a short entry to this particular adventure, so make of that what you will. As part of the research for this publication I did go to the Crooked Billet (still standing today, though possibly not the quaint 17th-century establishment that Hone describes elsewhere in the book). I am saddened to report that no drunk women presented me with a hag-stone, no matter how nicely I asked.

The Face in the Wall

Towards the entrance of the Crystal Palace Park there is a large bridge, almost an aqueduct in shape and structure. Those walking on the left-hand side on the park approach will find themselves walking beneath this bridge, marvelling at the engineering. It is indeed a feat, comparable to some of the architecture one might expect to find in the city itself. There is also the curious addition of the face of a woman in the brickwork. A mould of some kind, set in stone, she is pretty, and when I was taken to it by a friend, she was smiling, content.

My friend remarked that it was unusual to find her in such a way. 'She is changeable, though the manner in which her expression changes, and her reasons for doing so, are still unknown.'

I found this amusing, and over the next several days, made a point of walking to the bridge and noting any changes. My friend was correct. Smiling is a rare occurrence for our lady in the wall. Below, is a list of her emotional state on each day.

A slight grimace, as though smelling rotten food.

Anger. Plain and simple. Her eyes like daggers.

Bored and listless. I was compelled to touch her head and tell her that everything would be fine, before recognising the false nature of the face and walking away.

A scream, mouth open in agony.

The mechanism by which this is achieved I do not know. Only later did my friend tell me a story about the adulterous wife of the bridge architect, and how he buried her alive in his own structure. I have found no evidence to support this story and believe my friend to simply be taking advantage of my own dumb nature.

There is no face. Never was. What did he see?

Nothing. That's what he saw. Do I have to spell it out for you? Another one of Hone's inventions with this made up 'friend' giving him the willies. As for bricking someone up in a bridge? I've no idea. That story is new to me, and I'm guessing to you too. There's nothing about it in any local history books. In fact, the architect who designed the bridge appears to have been a lovely fellow, who had quite the obsession with sketching birds (if the British Museum give me permission perhaps I shall enclose some illustrations of his in this publication, they really are quite charming).

One thing that does bother me. 'What did he see?' That's what our unknown commentator writes in the margins. I assume that Hone saw nothing, but why does our annotator believe that he did? It's really rather odd.

The Hole in the Park

Whilst the Crystal Palace Park is being built and excavations are underway, I was invited on a private walk of the foundations by Sir Joseph Paxton. It's a marvellous site and the final exhibition will be something to behold.

As I was returning back towards Penge, about halfway across the park, I spied two men digging a hole. They did not appear to be part of the construction of the Palace so I took it upon myself to investigate their doings. As I approached, one of them (an older, grey-bearded gentleman) tapped the other (younger, entirely bald) on the shoulder.

'Who goes there?' the younger one said. He had a shovel in his hand, which he held aloft as though it were a weapon.

'My name is William Hone,' I replied. 'I have just been on a tour around the Palace construction. Tell me, are you part of it?' Knowing full well they were not.

'Indeed we are not, Sir.' The elder one spoke now. Irish.

'Well tell me then, what is it you are doing down here?'

The dirt on their clothing made it clear they had been digging for hours.

'We are digging to make our way home, Sir. Back to hell where we belong.'

'To hell?'

'Yes.' This time, the younger one spoke. 'For that is our home.'

Then they turned from me and continued their digging. I took another step forward. We were alone in the field, the three of us, and I could hear the distant sounds of the Crystal Palace being brought to life, but they seemed far further away than I believed they were. I was curious. What would I see were I to look in the place they had been digging? Would I be able to see hell itself?

A loud noise from behind startled me, and I turned to look. A parakeet flew overhead, its feathers brimming with colour.

I turned back to the two gentlemen, but they were gone, as too was the hole. But where it had once stood, a mound of freshly turned soil lay.

I have marked the spot. Hell this way. It is the path there. I have seen her crawl from it. I have seen her at night in the park. She lives between the spaces.

Difficult though it is to trace the steps of a man from over a century ago (not least the steps of a man who has clearly made half this stuff up), I ventured into the park and made my way to the sports centre which sits in the middle of it. Beneath the concrete steps, along the curve of the athletics stadium, there is indeed a spot where black graffiti reads *Hell this way*, an arrow pointing downwards into the tarmac of the car park. Our annotator has been busy, it seems. Perhaps he lives nearby even now.

I explored the area of course and the graffiti appears to be just that. It's a quaint touch but with no real purpose other than to frighten. I'll admit that it did a number on me at first, finally faced with a tangible connection between the writing and the real world. It was as though I was falling through the air, only to find myself clutching hold of a ledge and hauling myself to safety. The paint is faded though still there. (This may mean nothing; I contacted Bromley council and asked about how regularly they clean the graffiti from the park and got a lengthy history lesson about land disputes between the council and the private company who own the athletics stadium.) Perhaps these notes are far fresher than I first considered.

What do we make of 'She lives between the spaces', then? There are a number of references to a 'she' in his notes, never properly attributed, as though we should all be aware of exactly who 'she' actually is. At first I imagined her to be a scorned lover, or a deceased family member. But there is an ethereal quality to the references. As though she is in existence somewhere and he has evidence of this, but that the somewhere she exists is an impossible place. He has seen her at night in the park; I see people all the time in the park, so why is it important to note that he has seen her, unless the act of seeing her there is so strange, so uncanny, that it has moved him to write?

As for the two men digging their way to hell. The well-regarded Scottish folklorist Gerard McIntyre has a similar version that dates back somewhere to the 16th century. Long before Hone gave his rendition. McIntyre's version is, of course, far more interesting. In that, the gentleman follows the two men into hell, whereupon his stomach is slit open by the Devil, and stuffed with freshly caught fish. I imagine Hone would have had some continuity errors should he have pursued the more viscous threads of that particular narrative.

The Séance

We were asked by Madame Bedford to acquire a small map of the village and to spend our day walking the streets, in whatever direction we felt most natural. As we walked, we should draw our path on the map with a pencil (later to be inked in). I found myself drawn to the Thick Wood Road, which lies next to the park. It is a rather charming road in the daylight. Leafy and with some extraordinary houses for the area. Quite as soon as I reached the last house, just prior to the bridge, I felt an urge to knock on the door, though I dismissed it. Instead, I turned back down the road, walking this time on the park side of the road. When I reached the end, I felt myself drawn back in to the village.

There were three of us who attended the séance with Madame Bedford. Myself, Terence (an old pal from University, now rather well regarded in the armed forces), and Poppy (an old flame). We each presented our maps to Madame Bedford, who took them in turn, held them under candlelight, and copied the patterns of our journeys onto fresh sheets of paper.

'These are protective sigils,' she explained, passing them back to us, along with a pin. 'You will wear them at all times during the séance.'

My own sigil, a representation of my walk from earlier that morning, looked exceptionally uncomplicated compared to my two companions. A thick L shape (though reversed). Still, it was not the complexity of the symbol that mattered but the creation of it.

We sat together at a small table in Terence's dining room in his house on Anerley Road. He had dimmed the lights in advance, at Madame Bedford's instruction.

She is a curious woman, well known in Penge for hosting these events and communing with the spirit realm. Several people have sworn to me that they have witnessed things they cannot in their lives explain using any scientific method. She is diminutive but commands the presence of a public speaker. I dare say she could host quite the gathering should she wish, but three people is her maximum allotment and no more.

The other oddity is her complete lack of props. I have borne witness to several mediums before, all of whom relied upon cheap trickery and gimmicks to keep up pretences. The last one (before I swore off the practice completely) used some cheesecloth on a stick and a stuffed glove to give the appearance of an otherworldly presence. We hounded her right out of Farringdon the moment the ruse was discovered.

Not so with Madame Bedford. Our bodies, and our now pinned sigils, were all she required.

We each held hands in the circle, and this was not to be broken.

Almost instantly, Madame Bedford fell into a strange trance. Her head tilted back as though the muscles had just given way and she began to speak. The language which came out of her mouth was not one that I recognised and after what followed I will not curse myself by writing any form of it down on the page.

The room, which once seemed so large, suddenly felt small. As though the walls were closing in on us. Poppy tried to let go of my hand, but I held it tight, knowing we could not break the circle. Terence too looked frightful, but this was not to do with the changing size of the room. No. His expression of fear was directed just behind me, above my shoulder. I felt a chill. Something passed me by, teasing the back of my head. Another person, stroking their hand through my hair.

I did not turn around. I will admit that much.

'Why did she smile for you?' Poppy was the one who spoke. I have to admit, I was expecting it to be Madame Bedford, but she was still unconscious. 'Why did she smile for you when she will never smile for another?' Poppy's eyes were white and her voice... I cannot begin to describe her voice, except to say that it belonged to another.

It ended quite as quickly as it began. Madame Bedford woke, Poppy went back to her usual self (with no memory, it appears, of the events that transpired), and we departed rather hastily.

I am unlikely to forget this night.

She smiled for me too. Never forget that. She smiled for me. Still does. Still smiles. She is smiling now. I don't know why she comes to me, why I find her in the corners of this place when no one else can. It is as though she is trapped. This place is a boundary of the city but it is porous. There are people who are trapped within its walls. She is one.

But why is she happy?

There are many stories about Madame Bedford, and you likely know of most of them. 1855 or thereabouts would have put her in her early forties, and she traded as a medium all the way up until her terrible death in 1901. It was during one of her famed séances that she passed away, quite magnificently. Several patrons of hers who were in attendance at that session could have sworn that they saw her soul leave her body, and more still believe that she died after imparting several prophesies to the guests, at least one of which is said to have predicted the death of our dear Princess Diana (who was sixty years away from being born).

Still, though, this may well be one of Hone's less fanciful tales. Madame Bedford kept a remarkable series of accounts, naming all of her patrons (which included notable music hall performers, MPs and several members of the royal family), among which Hone does number. His visit is indeed listed as being in Penge, and is dated 3rd October 1854. His account of what he experienced is, to all intents and purposes, roughly in line with the accounts of anyone else who witnessed the medium's performance (and mark my words, it was very much a performance), with one glaring exception. This whole business of his old flame Poppy (presumably Poppy Beldringham, inheritor of the Beldringham vegetable oil business) speaking during the séance, and the things she said to him were, it seems, unique to his experience. Of course, it could all just be another elaboration (the man is known for it). Surely this is a tired narrative device, forcing us to make a connection between the smiling woman in the wall and this. Only a fool would fall for such nonsense.

Which brings me neatly on to our annotator, who has fallen hook, line, and – alas – sinker for this glaringly obvious fictional choice. This 'she' that he refers to could well be the woman in the wall, though as I say, the notes do not make it clear one way or the other.

Nevertheless, he is right about one thing. This place is at the end of something. Just the other day I was at an event in the British Library and introduced myself to a pretty young thing studying at a desk. When I told her I was researching in Penge she gave me a look as though I'd said I was living on Mars. What a world.

The Ghost of the King's Hall

I reel from nightmares that I have sustained over the past few days. In them, I walk the streets of Penge in the day, people pass me by and I wave, doff my hat, say 'good day' to them, but they do not hear or see me. I reach out to touch one woman who brushes past me, but my hand cannot reach her petticoat. It is as though something is separating the two of us. We occupy the same space, we are on the same street, and yet we couldn't be more distant.

On Wednesday, Poppy invited me to attend the King's Hall to see a rather charming bill of performers. Chief amongst them was a Martin McAdams, a hefty tub of a man with a wealth of bawdy jokes. I can honestly say I have never heard such things said in public before.

However, midway through the evening, just as a troupe of dancers took to the stage, I noticed a presence lurking just behind the curtain at stage right. A lone woman in a white dress, watching the dancers. She was not dressed as the dancers were, nor did she seem to be a part of their act. I turned my attention back to the dancers and when I looked back at the curtain, the woman was gone.

After the dancers were finished, and the audience applauded, I looked across the crowd, expecting to see Terence somewhere amongst them. He was not, but the woman was. She was sitting on the balcony, the same as me, though at the far end. Whilst everyone in the crowd was clapping and cheering, she remained silent. Whilst everyone watched the stage, her attention was directed solely at me.

Then I felt it again. The hand in my hair. Poppy was seated next to me, her hands on her lap. I turned to look to the row behind me and there she was. The woman in white.

Just as soon as I had seen her, she disappeared before my eyes, and I was left trembling in my seat.

After the show, I spoke to a Mr Denton, who owns and manages the King's Hall. I told him my story and asked him about any reported sightings of ghosts. He was not aware of any, nor of any deaths that have occurred in the venue, though he did seem rather excited about the possibility.

Mum said she'd come back. Said she'd take me. Didn't realise it would be like this. I hear her on the other side of doors, scratching at my window at night. I see glimpses of her on the night bus. Sat in the row behind me, watching. The blind spot of my vision is where she [hides]. She chose us. Our family. She [whispers] to me when I'm in bed. 'Every place here must lose someone.' London is

**a city full of people who get lost. I have been chosen. I will be [lost]
next. There is just one thing for it. The book must burn. It must be
destroyed.**

I so hope our mysterious annotator got the help he needed. My
transcription loses something in its transference, but at this point in
the text his handwriting is scratched and difficult to read. I may well
have written some of those words down incorrectly. It is my belief that
this book has caused him to lose his mind entirely. I dare say it has
been affecting me a little too. During my time researching this, I have
taken many trips down on the orange line to Penge and have walked
the streets, noting my thoughts. Iain Sinclair never made it this far
south for his book so I may well be the first of my kind to provide a
chronicle. I was walking under the bridge, past the place where Hone
says he saw the woman's face in stone, when I could have sworn I saw
a woman dressed all in white, passing me, smiling. She was just there
in the corner of my eye. An odd thing. I instinctively smiled back (I am
very much in tune with other people's body language) and yet, when I
made a point of introducing myself, it transpired there was no woman
at all.

Whatever fictions Hone was concocting, we can at least admit that
he was indeed a very good storyteller.

But the King's Hall, you ask. Well now. It may well have been Hone
who reported the existence of a ghost within its walls, but Frederick
Denton, manager of the place, took it upon himself to create a much
more lavish backstory for their spook. In around 1856 he began touring
groups backstage during the day, advertising it as a chance to spot the
'infamous ghost boy of Penge'. A far cry from the woman in white that
Hone spoke of. In an account of the tour, Peter Lynch (a resident of
Dulwich and noted diarist) commented that the boy was 'often heard
crying behind the curtain'. Mr Denton claimed the boy died during
the building's construction, blinded by an explosion caused by theatre
lighting. 'He can never see the wonderful productions put on at the
King's Hall and his crying is a result of his missed opportunities.'
Mr Denton then handed out discounted tickets to that evening's
performance.

I think you can all imagine what I make of that.

Impossible Room

I walked the Thick Wood Road again yesterday. I keep doing that and I cannot tell you why. I wish I knew. There have been days where I find myself waking up in the road there, as though coming out of a trance. The shadows on that road do not operate the same way as other roads. The sun moves differently. The Thick Wood Road is a strange phenomenon unto itself.

Terence walked with me up it to show me the house on the corner. Number 52. It is an impressive building, a three-storey townhouse which would do very comfortable for a family. I remarked as such to him and he laughed. 'I would never move in to this house,' he replied, and proceeded to show me why.

We walked around the building several times and as we did, Terence asked me to count the rooms. I counted six on the ground floor, including what appeared to be the entrance hallway. A dining room, a good-sized living room, a parlour, a kitchen, and a small study off to the side. Terence agreed with me, but asked me to count several more times just to be sure. Each time I found I got the same result.

We returned to Terence's house and took tea. As we were drinking, Terence produced a design for the house, and laid it on the table. He pointed at the plans for the ground floor. 'Count the rooms,' he said, 'double count them if you wish.' I did. The plans only accounted for five rooms. The small study was not on the plans.

'But of course, the owners simply built a small extension to the property. Perhaps they came into some money.'

'The house has been empty ever since the building was completed. I have taken a tour of it myself. The sixth room does not exist.'

'Then they built it and forgot to install a door.'

'The house ends before the study. It is an impossible room.'

I had to see it for myself, and so two days later I took a tour of the house with a solicitor under the guise of a potential buyer. The house was warm, an odd thing for a property that has never been lived in. The entrance hall was as it appeared to be from the outside, and to the left, two doorways led to the living and dining rooms. At the end of the hallway, another door opened up into the kitchen and parlour. I walked into the parlour, for that is where the entrance to the study ought to be. It was as Terence suggested. The wall of the parlour had no other doorway in, and yet, it was at the edge of the house. I looked out of the window and found myself stood in the exact place the study could be seen from the outside.

A most curious piece of magic which delighted me, though in the days since I have been waking up to find myself in the garden, watching the impossible room. Something inside me tells me that someone is there.

She wouldn't let me burn it. Instead she showed me everything. I have found the doorway, it was in my house all along. It has been locked for so long. I should never have opened it. She will be coming tonight. I know it.

Here's where it gets interesting. The Thick Wood Road is now Thicket Road, and almost all of the houses that stood there in 1850 or so are still standing now. I took a trip up that road just the other day researching this particular element and found number 52 standing exactly as it did. It's been converted into a number of flats now, and none of their occupants were in when I buzzed for their attention.

However, the gate to the garden was open and, copying Hone's own actions, I made my way around the perimeter of the property, counting the rooms. Their purposes have all changed in the last century, but as with Hone, I too counted six rooms. In fact, stranger still, next to what used to be the parlour (now a tiny second bedroom adjacent to the kitchen) there is a bizarrely Victorian-esque study. I took my phone out to snap a quick photo of the room, and as I looked into the screen to line up the shot I noticed a quick wisp of white, the edge of a dress disappearing out of view. I ran back around to the front of the property and buzzed again. No answer, which was frustrating. I realise now that this may well be the house belonging to our annotator. When he says that he has found the doorway, perhaps he has finally found his way into this mysterious room. My, how exciting a find would that be? A completely preserved space. Though the fact that I have not read about this anywhere would suggest that he was unsuccessful in his search. A pity.

The Thick Wood Road

I returned again to the house on the Thick Wood Road. I was told by Poppy of a black dog with demonic red eyes who can be seen crawling beneath the roots of a tree somewhere near Sydenham and I fully intended to go there and investigate, but instead I found myself in the garden of 52 Thick Wood Road staring at the impossible room.

I can feel her watching me. She is within the room. A candle flickers and shadows dance on the walls, though there is no doorway. Even when I am not in the garden I can picture it in my mind. Perhaps she is locked within me, and I too have an impossible room within. A part of my brain locked away. A doorway in the mind I cannot open. What secrets are within?

Some time after visiting the garden, on the walk up the road, I was welcomed into another house. I cannot tell you the name of the house, nor the number. Something compels me not to. They saw me wandering the road and beckoned I come to them lest some of the darker elements of the neighbourhood spy me and take advantage. 'Many men have lost their lives walking the Thick Wood,' the woman who opened the door to me said.

Their house is bedecked with herbs and plants. The furniture is old and discoloured, though none of the women appeared to be much older than I. There are eight of them living here, they told me.

'Stay for a drink, dear fellow,' they whispered. I hastened to say to them that I could not. That I was meeting an old friend and that I was expected. That was a lie; something within me compelled me to lie to them.

'You were in the garden again.' Another of the eight spoke from the shadows. 'You have been in that garden before. You will be in that garden again.'

'Just one drink,' the youngest of the women said. She had a cup already prepared. It smelled so sweet. But I stood and made my way to the door. 'I am not thirsty, and my friend is waiting,' I explained.

'Did you see her in the room? She smiled for you. She smiled and welcomed you.'

'Welcomed me where?' I did not mean to engage them on the topic but in that moment my voice did not belong to me.

Two of the women were stood behind the chair I sat in, and they leant forwards, and began stroking my head. Another laughed, a giggle really. Childish, but loaded.

'Please drink, Sir.' The youngest again. She took my hand and prised open my palm, placing the cup within it and closing my fingers around it tight. 'You are so terribly thirsty.'

I got up, dropping the cup. The women stepped back, all of sudden afraid, though I did nothing to frighten them.

'I must go this instant.'

At that moment there was a knock at their door. I am saved! *I thought, believing Terence had come to my rescue. This could not have been the case though, as he had no idea where I was at that moment. A stupid thought from a desperate mind.*

'You cannot go,' the youngest said. 'She has come to you and she has so much to show you.'

And so I sat back down and I thought about Penge. I thought about how it is a place for hiding yourself, perhaps hiding so well that you can lose yourself entirely.

I hope not to lose myself to this place.

There are things that fall through the gaps, like her. Please, if this book can pass across, hear my warning. There is magic in this place. But it is a hungry magic and it has tasted me and found me succulent. I am trapped and I can never leave. She would never let me.

This is the last entry. I honestly don't know what it is about this book, but it does cause the mind to play tricks. I came to Penge on Tuesday for a day of research. I visited the impossible house on Thicket Road, and walking up, I tried to peer at the other houses to see if I could spot the house in which Hone ended his tale. I was unsuccessful, as I expected, and took a walk in the park instead.

The park is very different from the days of Hone. Gone is the Crystal Palace itself, which was still being built at the time of writing. Instead, the ruins host council mandated firework displays, food markets, and the occasional circus. The concrete behemoth that is the sports centre and athletics stadium sit in the middle of it all, where before Hone would have encountered grass and greenery. Next to one of the lakes, there is a curiosity that still remains from Hone's period. A number of dinosaur statues, scientifically iffy but still impressive to look at. I found myself standing by them and waiting for hours. My mind wandered, my thoughts occupied by the stories I had been reading from Hone's book.

It was only when I noticed the sun going down that I decided to leave, and I went to the station to catch the next Overground home. But something inside me made me want to stay. I stood at the entrance to the station and I just could not bring myself to leave. I watched the train pull in and passengers disembark. I saw the doors close and the train head on back towards the city.

I will get a hotel tonight and get my mind in order. Hone is right about one thing. If you don't keep an eye on yourself, you can get very lost indeed.

|They Have Gone to the City|

~

Snide bastard charges them a tenner entry, like they haven't been coming here all their lives. Paul eyes the doorman up and down, goes to say, 'Don't you know who we are?' but stops short. Remembers how long it has been since they've last been here. Since they were last in Manchester. Since they were last together. Shit that it took this to bring them back home. He watches as James pulls out a couple of notes and pays for the two of them to get in. Fine. He can act the older brother all night if he wants to, especially if it means free drinks.

In the entrance of Satan's Hollow, he can hear the rain start pissing down outside. Typical. It never bothered him when he was a kid, but the weather is different down on the coast and the shock of coming back after all these years makes the drizzle feel harsher, like a beating. He tries not to take it personally.

'Remember when you caught Ben fucking that bird up the arse in the men's?' James laughs as they head down the steps into the club. Paul shakes his head. He doesn't. Not really. Those days are hazy trips, clouded with beer and cheap spirits, cheap weed too, sometimes other stuff. 'You ran out of the bog and told all of us. Remember?'

'Sorry, no.'

'You were such a dickhead back then.'

Back then, lots of people were telling him the same thing. His brother, his mates, Mum, the teachers, and yeah, maybe he was. But that's what he loved about a place like this. You could be a dickhead and a fuck-up. You could be a failure. You could be whatever the fuck outside, but in here it doesn't matter, because the music is here, and the pit is here. In the pit, you're all mates.

That's what they need tonight. To be mates again.

The place hasn't changed. Fake brickwork lines the walls, and the pillars holding the ceiling up are coated in plaster and painted to resemble lava flows. Iron gates surround a small booth by the bar. In the corner of the room, an enormous devil sculpture, its arms wide open and welcoming, oversees the dance floor.

The DJ has started out low-key tonight, a tune that Paul doesn't recognise until the vocals come in. High pitched and melodic: Coheed. Decent tune, he thinks. If the dance floor was busier, he'd probably get in there, but right now it's occupied by a single lanky goth kid spinning a keyring chain he probably got from Affleck's about a decade ago. He's got some moves.

What he wants is to hear something from his youth. Something old that makes him feel young again. Glassjaw or Thrice. Fuck, Thursday even. What he really wants the guy to play is some Triangle, but there's no chance they'd get a play in a place like this. Sometimes the guy in the punk room at Rockworld would throw on a tune or two, but that place is – what? – a Tesco now. Man, fuck this city.

The bar is dead. Always is before eleven. Paul checks his phone: half ten. They got here early partly to claim a seat before the crowds arrived, and partly because the city had felt so alien to them. Paul had a list in his head of the decent pubs and bars nearby, but he'd soon found them closed up or transformed beyond all recognition. They'd given up and come here. All the better, Paul thinks. He'd take any chance not to have to talk to his brother. Loud music, cheap drinks. Then maybe they can just pretend to be sixteen again, giddy kids showing fake IDs to bouncers who couldn't give a fuck. Coming home at three in the morning after walking along the tram line when the last bus kicked them off somewhere in Sale. Neither of them called those the glory days, but they knew full well what they were.

There's a girl leaning on a plastic pallet in the corner of the bar, Satan's tee tied around her waist. Her brown hair is shaved on one side but hangs down past her shoulders on the other. She looks familiar to Paul, but he can't put his finger on it. Probably just clocked her when he came in. His memory got shot once he turned thirty.

Coheed segues into a Something She tune from before they started churning out whiney ballads. This is more like it.

Paul makes for the dance floor, but James holds him back.

'Come on, man.'

'I'm not ready yet.'

He said the same thing outside the solicitor's office, the two of them sat in the waiting room. Paul wasn't ready either, but they had to do it. They were the only ones left. When he'd heard their names being called, Paul got up and made for the door, but James didn't budge.

'I can't.'

The first time Paul could remember his older brother with no confidence, no swagger, no bravado. First time he'd ever seemed like a little boy.

'She's all we had. If she's got words for us then we owe it to her to listen.'

James never wanted to listen. He wanted the music to drown it all out.

Without Paul noticing, the place fills up. Throngs of students get in just before the entry fee goes up, crowding round the bar for vodka or whisky with a dash of Coke. Knocking them back. A group of tall goths stand around one of the tables near the DJ, huddled together like they're conducting a séance. The girl from behind the bar weaves her way through the patrons, picking up empties. Paul nurses his third beer. The queue at the bar's too long to bother with a fourth.

Where is James?

Ever since he got the call about their mum, a vein of worry has been alive in his body. A nerve that had always been there but never touched. He doesn't have kids, but if he did, he'd be terrified every minute of their lives, watching out for hazards on the roads, sharp objects, and water. Especially the water.

That's where they'd found her. Under the Deansgate locks, fished out by two bouncers who thought she was a punter from their bar who'd fallen in. She'd been floating there for a week at least. He'd sat through the coroner's report, excruciating as it was, because he had to know it all. All the horrible details. The final moments of her life.

She was their mum. It was only right.

There were things he didn't understand: why had she been walking the canals so late at night? How had she fallen in? There were things the coroner tried to make sense of: how had she managed to swallow all those objects? Cigarette butts and discarded chips, sure, but the pieces of cotton, like soggy clouds, that they pulled from her stomach? That still didn't sit right with Paul. Nor did the eventual decision: an accident.

James wouldn't go to the court. He wasn't ready, so Paul went for the two of them, primed himself with the details in case James ever wanted to know.

He sometimes found their relationship odd. That he was the sensible one, the organiser, and James the quiet one. He'd always thought that it should be the other way round. There were moments where he thought James believed that too, and would break out of that shell. Mostly in places like this.

Another song breaks through his thoughts. At the Drive-In. Immediately, two white guys, both the spit of Cedric Bixler-Zavala, take to the dance floor, heads and afros thrashing to 'One Armed Scissor'. Now he wants to join them, to give in to the music and let go, but he knows the reaction he'd get from James if he went up there alone. At a time like this, they need to stick together.

He orders another beer and leans against the bar, the sticky remnants of spilled shots immediately making him regret his decision.

Where is his brother? In the loo chatting with the Rasta handing out kitchen roll and dosing everyone with cheap aftershave? Outside maybe, nabbing a spliff from some fresher? He'll come back.

'You okay, mate?' He feels a tap on his shoulder. The Glass Collector is stood behind the bar.

'Sorry, am I in your way?'

She starts speaking, but he can't hear her, so he leans in and she shouts to make herself heard. 'You just looked lost in thought. I saw you earlier too. Not dancing?'

'Not ready. Doesn't feel right.'

She's a great deal younger than him, that's clear up close where he can see the freshness of her face, no greys in her hair. She's got old eyes though, like she's seen some shit. Most people who work behind a bar do. She's a kid. But then, so many people here are. He's the one out of place here, him and James. They came here hoping to feel something. *Youth*, he thinks. He wanted nothing more than to be dragged into the past. Into Manchester twenty years ago, when things were easy. When the two of them could be fuck-ups and no one cared. When they could act like they owned the place.

Looking at her reminds him that it's all past now. She runs her hand through the shaved side of her head. For a brief moment he thinks he can smell the canal, the stink of stagnant water and litter.

'You know,' he says, 'I used to come here years ago.'

'I know,' she replies. Of course she does, why else would he be here?

'Place never changes, music, the crowd… it's all just as it was.' The smell is different though. Back before the smoking ban you couldn't smell the sweat or the spilled beer. That's all. 'You'd fit right in back then, you know?'

He hears how it sounds before the sentence comes out of his mouth: slurred with beer, painfully flirtatious. He doesn't mean it like that. She's not even twenty for fucks' sake, and he really doesn't want to be the creepy old man in the club hitting on the kids behind the bar. He knew enough of those guys back in the day.

'Sorry,' he says to her. 'Didn't mean it like that.'

Whatever song that had been playing fades, and in its place he hears the familiar opening to a Frozen Gold tune he can't remember the name of. They used to play this one ages ago and, just like back then, the dance floor empties. The Glass Collector is gone, no doubt off to do her job. Why this surprises Paul he doesn't know. Maybe because she walked off so quickly, but then who wants to spend their night chatting to him? He looks out at the crowds, but he can't see her. She blends in so well. James isn't there either, as far as he can see.

Cheap beer stirs uneasily in him, and he staggers back towards the toilets. He tries to recall the night James talked about, when Paul caught Ben in the loos with that girl, but the memory isn't there, just the story. The past, he used to think, was a disease. You catch it when you're young, and it sits in your body infecting every single cell. When you're older, it blooms and bursts. Pustules of pus and past exploding out. People catch the past all the time. Now he has it too. For a long time he wanted no part of it. But now, the way things have gone, he so desperately wants to embrace it. He wants to remember that night, all the nights. Remembering them keeps them alive, and then, maybe, she could be alive again too. *I am diseased* he thinks, and smiles.

Inside the toilet, the stink of aftershave is strong. The guy handing out the loo roll hums 'Three Little Birds'. The cubicles are all empty, and Paul mumbles an apology before turning around again.

Outside is the same. No sign of his brother, just the cold Manchester air, thick with smoke. The rain falls from clouds that resemble soggy cotton wool. He recalls a night years ago. Mad one. Breaking into the abandoned Post Office depot in Alty through a smashed window in the sorting office. It had been a cotton mill once, shuttered and converted and now closed again. Setting off fireworks indoors. Sparks flying, crackling. James laughing. Paul wandered off, kicking through yellowing post with his feet. Like autumn leaves, he'd thought. All those letters that will never get to their destination, just rotting on the floor, turning to mulch. It was as though there were people in those envelopes, little snippets of them, and he was kicking them, stomping on them. There was dust in the air. Breathing it in, he'd felt as though he was breathing in the history. The memories.

He'd reached the manager's office, uniform still hung up behind the door, when he heard James shout 'Fire!' with glee. Ran out to find flames licking at the furniture in the corner. A stray firework, a spark on the paper.

All those lives up in flames. In the end, it had been so easy.

They sat on the embankment in the wet grass and watched the building burn.

Another song. Snaps him right out of that memory so fast he can still feel the heat of the fire on him. The dance floor is packed again. Fucking heaving with people. Disturbed's 'Down With The Sickness' echoes around him, the infectious *oh-wah-ah-ah-ah* of the song chanted by everyone in there. And there, weaving in and out of the dancers, is James. Sweaty and dead-eyed. On something, Paul recognises, a little jealous.

He makes his way through the crowd, half pushing-half dancing, but when he reaches the spot where he saw his brother, he finds someone else. He looks around, stops for a moment, only to be jostled by moshers lashing out. 'Come on, move,' he mutters but no one can hear him. In his ear, someone screams along to the tune. He pushes his way back out, turns around to look at the dance floor and all he sees are ghosts of the past dancing, infecting each other. He came here for that, the hit of history, but this is stale. It's an old memory, preserved, not right. Now his brother is somewhere and he doesn't know where, and their mum… he shoves that thought down, deep down. Not time to think about that. Not tonight.

The song winds down and now, what is it? Something he recognises. Is it a song? No, not quite. It's something else. The sound of a city. Traffic and people. A distant siren. People are still dancing, and over his shoulder he catches movement. He turns quick. James, heading off to the smoking area, arm around some girl. She looks like the Glass Collector, but she can't be.

Paul pushes through a group of people and follows.

They couldn't decide on what to do with her. She left no instructions and burial seemed far too expensive for them. Someone suggested cremation and they went with it, the ashes stored in a small cardboard box. James wanted to take her up to Winter Hill and scatter them to the wind, but Paul couldn't understand why. She had never been there, never been one for walking either. But she had loved her city. He imagined standing on top of the Beetham Tower, gusts licking at him, holding the box aloft and opening it, letting the ashes scatter to the air. Below, people would open their mouths and the ashes would fall and catch on their tongues like snowflakes.

She would live inside all of them.

A glimpse of his brother in the smoking area, whistling between two lads sharing a joint and a kiss. A flittering idea of him that passes through the space. He was here, it says, but no longer. The girl is nowhere to be seen either.

Inside then.

What is that song? It doesn't sound like any kind of music to him, just a cacophony of noise. He still hears the city, but now there are layers on top of layers. Animals screaming. People. Screeching and crying. And something deep down in the back of it, something he cannot put his finger on. There is no rhythm but when he looks to the dance floor, the crowd has found it and they are dancing wildly. Hair whipping over their faces, arms flailing, as though they are compelled.

There is no sign of his brother, but he spots the Glass Collector.

She is stood to the side of the dance floor, near the DJ. She appears unmoved by the music, or whatever the noise is. He nods at her.

He wanted to dance. That's why they came here. To move, be a part of the crowd, and feel part of the city again. Their mother loved it and they inherited that love. Without her tethering them to Manchester, they needed to remember. He tries moving to the noise of the city, tries moving in time with the rest of them, but he can't. They are in a different city to him.

Then she is next to him, though he cannot recall seeing her approach.

'I'm looking for my—' he starts to say, but then she is closer, lips nearly touching his. When she speaks, he feels her voice inside him: 'You can see her again. You can find him. They have gone to the city.' When she opens her mouth, he can see the rain dancing under streetlamps, hear the cacophonous horns of the trams. Here is the noise. They move to her music. Inside, the buildings grow tall, but they are old. Somewhere distant, he can hear the slow trickle of canal water through a break in the lock. She unlocks her jaw, her mouth growing wider and wider, and now he can feel it, the cold wintery wind of a Manchester night. There is rhythm in there, something he can feel in his bones. It moves him. He places his hands either side of her lips, grasping hold of her cheeks to give him a leg up, the cotton of her skin oddly abrasive against his fingers. And as he enters her, he thinks of one word. Home.

|Gods & Kings|

∽

They were protesting outside the hospital, and I saw Sean amongst the crowd as I headed home. I hadn't seen him in years, not since university. Thought he'd moved far away from home. Never expected him to get caught up in anything like this.

They were a small group. Just fourteen or fifteen, and they were cordoned off by police, behind tiny metal fences. I could recognise Sean, even without hair. The others? They were all the same. Skinheads. Not the same kind I remembered serving at the bar in Rockworld back up North. Those guys were kind, intelligent, shite dancers. This lot, it was as though they'd shaved it all off for anonymity. Safety in numbers. They were chanting horrible racist slogans. Yelling it in unison like they were at football. Like it was a game.

When I got home I told Martin.

'Sean? Seriously?'

'Crooked nose and all. It really threw me for one, you know?'

'Did he recognise you?'

The flat rumbled, pictures shaking, glasses in the cupboards tinkling as a bus passed by our room. We'd lived on the high street for three years and never got used to it.

'I don't think he saw me. I looked right at him and it was like he had blinkers on or something. Like he wasn't looking at anything, just another part of the mob.'

I thought back to University days, drinking cheap lager in the tatty garden of our house, Sean showing me how to smoke weed properly. Never realised I was doing it wrong. Always thought I was just immune. Stupid twat that I was. Had there been anything back then? A warning sign?

Long after Martin had fallen asleep I was still thinking back to when we'd lived together. The three of us. The peeling wallpaper, curled edges of carpets, empty lager cans strewn around the place. We'd had so much fun together, and yet, there he was, in front of the hospital.

I logged in to Facebook. Sean was still my friend on there at least, pushed to the bottom of some list by algorithms. I hadn't seen a post by him in years. His profile picture was taken from that day, him arm in arm with the other guys at the hospital, placards held in front of their chests, like slogans on a t-shirt.

SEND THEM HOME

NO FREE HEALTHCARE FOR TERRORISTS

KILL ISLAMIST SCUM

And they looked so happy.

I kept scrolling, throwing myself further back in time, tracing the path of his life backwards. He posted news articles almost daily, sometimes just stuff from the Mail, racist bullshit but nothing the rest of us didn't wind up reading somewhere, but then there were articles from other places. Worse places. Badly edited YouTube videos from angry kids all about no go zones in London, about how the Mayor was a secret terrorist infiltrator. How we were all doomed. All of them the same, little England flag avatars and pages named The Patriot Game, Albion Forever, Crusade 2.0.

Outside the barber's shop opposite, some kids were laughing, their muffled chuckles just about audible through the bedroom window. We never could get much sleep around here, but we loved it. Martin turned over on his pillow.

'Jake, are you still looking?' He didn't have his eyes open, and he half mumbled it, like he was still dreaming.

I kissed him and told him to get back to sleep.

I put my phone away but I couldn't get it out of my head. Sean had never been that kind of guy. He was a shy stoner from a small Essex town I'd never heard of until I moved to London. We all made fun of his accent in halls until we began to adopt pieces of it and our voices began to imitate and meld into that university accent everyone had. There are phrases of his that are mine now, the way he said 'shite' with so much emphasis on the 'eye' when he got frustrated. I do that now. All of us from university do.

They were back at the hospital again the next day. All of us who worked there got a warning by text telling us to use an alternative entrance. I ignored it.

The group was back, though fewer in number this time. Sean was still there, with about five others. The placards were out again, and they were chanting.

'Terrorist scum, terrorist scum,' some yelled.

Across from them, a counter protest had formed in larger numbers. Families with colourful signs in support of the NHS, and smiling emoticons. Others somewhere in amongst that crowd had darker messages for the skinheads, 'FUCK FASCIST SCUM' said one. On another, someone had stapled photos of Tommy Robinson, Katie Hopkins, and a few others I didn't recognise; they'd each been shot perfectly through the head with an air rifle, the tiny pellet holes perforating the banner. Below the photos, a message written in red, 'GUESS WHO'S NEXT?'

Between the two groups of protestors, police had formed a small corridor.

The counter-protestors cheered when I approached, waving their signs, but I veered across towards the skinheads. I wanted to show them I wasn't scared I suppose, but more than that, I wanted Sean to see me, to recognise me and have that same shock moment I did when I first saw him again after all the years. Maybe a shock like that would spring him out of whatever delusion he'd been caught up in.

Sean seemed quiet. He eyed me up as I walked past. Had he recognised me? I stopped, stood between two police officers and stared right at him.

'Jake?' he said, and stepped forward to the front of the group. 'You work here? You're treating that scum?'

I said nothing.

'Tell your terrorist scum friends that He's coming. We've said the words right and we've shown Him what this country is now, and He's angry and He's coming.'

Which side surged forward first? I don't know. One minute Sean was stood defiant and angry in front of me, the next, both sides of the protests clashed. The officers did their best, holding their hands out, trying to keep the two groups apart, but it was to no avail. I was shoved out of the way by someone, and I caught a glimpse of thick black numbers tattooed on the side of his face. As I staggered back, someone else barged into my shoulder and I fell to the floor. All around me, people shoved back and forth, placards clattered to the floor. People screamed meaningless slogans. I tried to back out of the melee, but as I did, I heard a punch that cracked the air, and one of the skinheads fell, blood seeping from his nose, staining the numbers tattooed on the side of his face.

More police showed up and a handful of people were hauled away.

The protests would continue, especially now one of their own was inside.

We were told not to talk to the media, or anyone else for that matter. A Sun reporter got caught, sitting in the waiting room, sneezing into a handkerchief and fishing for stories, hoping to get access to us. She'd been turfed out by security, but no-one could be sure she was the only one.

Our patients were recovering. None of us talked about whether they deserved to be treated. An oath is an oath, we all knew that. We were there to help people, not judge them. Morality didn't come into it. Let the police handle them.

The skinhead's name was Aaron. I checked in on him in the ward that afternoon. His concussion wasn't too bad, but the doctors wanted to be sure. When I approached him I could see he was groggy, but he was sat up watching some video on his phone. On the side of his face, he'd had the numbers 14 and 88 tattooed so that they curved around his eye, each number two or three inches in size. He was a wiry kid, lean and agitated. To me, he looked like a phone, constantly being bombarded with notifications, vibrating endlessly.

'How are you feeling?' I asked.

He looked up at me and it took a second for him to recognise me. 'You were out there today.'

'I was walking to work.'

'Whatever, you were talking to Sean, like you knew him.'

'How long has he been...' I struggled to find the word.

'Sean's been awake for longer than I have. Years maybe.'

Years.

I could remember a time back when we'd both been freshers, sinking the sixth shot of the night, laughing our arses off about something that I've forgotten about. Had it been there all along? A little knotted ball of bile, and hate, and all that shite.

Years.

'You one of the lot looking after *him?*'

'I can't talk about any other patients.'

He spat on the floor. 'Whatever happens, you've got it coming.'

Sean put up another photo that evening. It cropped up on my newsfeed this time, my trawling through his profile had bumped him up in significance. It was a snapshot from a Mirror journalist, a group of doctors walking into the building as the protestors screamed at them. Just looking at the photo you could practically still hear the chanting. It wasn't such a great photo though. Sean stood, fist in the air, mouth wide open, clear as day; but the man behind him, hand on his shoulder, he was blurred. Not even blurred so to speak, more like I knew he was there, but I couldn't see him. Like he was in some blindspot.

I got a text from a colleague, Aaron had bolted from the hospital. No surprise.

Outside, some kid on a moped raced around the block whilst Martin slept, and I stared at the ceiling, counting the squares in the pattern made by the plaster.

It felt like the whole city was just noise and tension except for there in that room where we lay.

They found the bodies in the morning and took the survivors to the hospital. I was rushed in.

Two of them were DOA, and the rest had gone straight into emergency surgery. One of the nurses who'd helped the paramedics bring them in was sat in the changing room, pale.

'They're not going to make it,' she finally got out.

It had been a mess.

The police had been called to some house up in Anerley, near the station, where the protestors had been living. Outside, splintered furniture was scattered across the front lawn along with broken glass from the now shattered windows. The door hung off its hinges. One officer, waiting for the last of them to die, told me it was like the aftermath of the worst explosion he had ever seen. Except there had been no explosion. Those who had died immediately had been thrown from the house into the street, the parts of them that were missing still being discovered months later, burying themselves in shrubs. Inside the house the others lay injured and dying, surrounding a cavernous hole in the centre of the living room.

They died, or most of them did anyway. Sean held on for a bit but it was clear he wasn't going to make it. I made a point of heading up to his ward to see him. He was awake but delirious, screaming and lashing out at whoever would come near him.

'Does he speak to you when you see him?' one of the consultants asked towards the end. She'd cornered me in the canteen. News had travelled around that I'd known the soon-to-be-deceased.

'He doesn't recognise me.'

'He spoke once, to one of the nurses on her rounds.'

'What did he say?'

'Nothing useful. Gibberish I suppose, but I thought it might make sense to you, since you knew him.'

'What was it?'

'We said the words wrong. Said it all wrong.' The consultant read from a report she had. 'Do you know what any of that could mean?'

'I've no idea. Sorry.'

On the bus home I scrolled through the newsfeed once again. Someone had hacked Sean's account, had posted dozens of updates since the attack. The same words over and over again. 'Richard came and judged me Richard came and judged me Richard came and judged me Richard came and judged me' and every time, the photo of them outside the front of the hospital, Sean's fist in the air, and that other person standing beside him, a ghostly double exposure.

There were more deaths, kids getting suspended from social media, promising retribution, but turning up dead themselves. It was an epidemic of violence. People blamed gangs. Organised violence is easier to understand. But it didn't feel organised.

Not in the same way at least.

One morning, I found myself walking up the street from Penge to Anerley, looking for the house that Sean had been living in with the others. Convincing myself I could find something where the police couldn't. The toxic smell of burning metal drifted from a factory on Oakfield Road, and I pushed through it up towards the station.

It was no different a house than any of the others, from the outside at least. Some brave estate agents were already trying to sell it, though the windows were boarded up and splintered furniture was embedded in the grass. It seemed foolish to think that someone would bother looking at it, let alone offer to buy it, but then I dismissed that. It would go almost immediately and in a few months, some new flats would spring up in its place. People like me and Martin would move in.

The boards covering the back door gave way easily and I stepped inside.

I was in the kitchen. Nothing had been cleaned up or moved since the police had been here. Mugs sat on the countertops, the milk rotten and green. There were traces of fingerprint powder smeared on the door handles, fridge doors, around bloodied footprints. A rotten smell hung in the air, uneaten food and rising damp from the floorboards. Something, somewhere, was leaking. Black mould coated the walls, though it looked like no kind of mould I had seen before. It looked as though it was growing, living inside the walls, but the texture and colour was that of a burn. As though somewhere beneath the plaster and brickwork, the house was on fire.

Through the kitchen door, a short corridor leading to the front door, stairs to the left. To the right, a door, blasted off its hinges, hanging awkwardly. More mould growing along the walls, bleeding through the plaster. I picked my feet over more footprints, and broken wood, and stepped through the shattered doorway into the living room.

Water bubbled up from a broken pipe somewhere within the crater in the centre of the room. A dining table and chairs would have sat there, and now the chairs had shot out, like shrapnel, their metal legs embedded in the walls and TV. Half of the dining table had exploded upwards, now teetering worryingly in the ceiling. Where the other half was, I couldn't tell.

All around the crater, markings had been scratched into the floor, writing and symbols that I didn't recognise.

I took a step towards the crater, and I felt something within it. A kind of power lurking beneath the surface. Deep within me I felt a burning anger, an alien emotion rising. The wet, cavernous smell of fungus and rotting wood was suffocating, and I had to leave.

Outside the house I felt the blackness of the walls and the power from within the crater, even just from the gate. I felt it follow me until the fumes from the warehouse nearby overcame me, and I coughed my way to the station.

Just a handful of people came to Sean's funeral. I stood at the back, distant from whatever he had become. His mum and dad, who I remembered vaguely, sat tearful at the front. They stood to say some words about how much they loved him, how much of a tragedy this was. He was so young. So much potential.

Someone else spoke after. The kid from the hospital, Aaron. Eyes dry and raw, he looked out across the people in the church.

'I'm sorry,' he said, already leaving the pulpit. 'I can't.'

I found him outside smoking.

'You were there, weren't you?'

'I don't know what you're on about.'

'It doesn't matter now, does it? You're dead. He's coming for you anyway and you can't stop it.' Shameful to admit, but I felt a small amount of glee saying that to him.

'We said it wrong, or, or the things in the book were wrong. He was our Saint. He was our God. Our King. He was going to protect us, lead us in the war. But it wasn't him.'

But it had been him, hadn't it? The thing they brought back. It was right. It worked.

'Did he say anything, when he came out of the ground?' I asked the kid, but he shook his head. No.

'Just looked at us. Each of us. I can still see him looking at me. His eyes, I remember his eyes. Like they were alien. Like they didn't understand what I was.'

He dropped his cigarette and stubbed it out clumsily, grinding his foot into the pavement. I looked down at the ground and I saw them then, the dead, ground up and spread amongst the soil and the shit, and the concrete that made this city. I saw them buried and turned to face us. Always watching.

Aaron would die before the week was through. His broken body fished out of the canal near King's Cross. It made the news, though barely. The night I read about it, I couldn't sleep. I left Martin in bed and I put my shoes on and left the flat. It is never quiet in London. The night buses, full of people, shuttled past. Kids sat in front of the barber shop, smoking and laughing. The burnished red of a fox tail whipped past me into a driveway. My feet felt heavy as I walked, my soles tramping on the tarmac, but I carried on up the road, trudging on the upturned faces of the dead, their eyes wide open, staring.

|Stabbed in the Neck by Dot Cotton|

~

The Corridor, First Floor
The building wakes.

Flat 102
There is a dinner party. The house smells of cooked meats and dead grapes. Lights are dimmed low. The table in the dining room is so full that people are perched on the edges, stretching forward to take a bite from their food. Occasionally someone laughs, but the building doesn't understand the joke, or it misses it, having concentrated too much on something someone else was saying. One of the women is engrossed in her phone, and when she hits send on a message the building spies (   ) and it thinks that it might have found something, but it is fleeting.

'How would you want to go then Mike?' It's a man speaking. He's got both hands held out and he's louder than the others. When he speaks, the rest go quiet and listen. 'We were talking the other day,' he continues, 'about how we'd like to die, if we were in a soap, and Mike, you never answered.'

'What was yours then?' Someone from the end of the table. The head? The building has always confused ends.

'Simple. Bathtub. Radio. Evil twin brother.'

Everyone finds that very funny.

'He'd have a goatee then?' Head.

Everyone finds that very funny.

'So what would yours be then Mike?' Someone else.

Mike is sat in the middle of a cluster of people. He is sipping a beer. Everyone else has wine and he looks embarrassed. Stares down at his beer as though, if he concentrated enough, the liquid inside would expand and spill out of the glass and engulf the room, drowning everyone. Somewhere in the building, there is a excited flurry of air. The building cannot tell whether Mike would want to sink with the rest, or float.

Mike, the building determines, might be the candidate.

'Yeah.' Someone else. 'How would you want to die?'

Mike looks up. 'Stabbed in the neck by Dot Cotton.'

Everyone finds that very funny.

The building, as most things are allowed to do, changes its mind about Mike. He is perhaps not ideal. Its eye drifts.

Flat 431

There are two of them here. A man and a woman. They are drinking. No, they are drinkers. Constant and repetitive. Drinking implies a stopping point, that at once they will have drunk and it will end. This, the building knows, will not happen. They are a figure-eight loop of boozing. Like a still photo. Here, the building feels ruined and isolated.

It moves on.

Flat 322

The children play with the ghost of a boy. He tells them how he went underneath the machines one day to fix a loose bolt and was caught and dragged in and killed. The children laugh, and don't quite understand. The boy doesn't mind. He has friends now. They play hide and seek in the tiny flat, the boy flinging open cupboards and throwing cutlery around when he can't find them. He picks up their toys and dolls and they glide through the air. The children hide under the sofa. They always hide under the sofa. Sometimes they wonder why the boy doesn't just come straight to the sofa, because it's where they always are. Sometimes they think the boy likes to throw things, to break plates and clatter pans. Once, when they had rolled themselves up inside the living room curtains, he threw all of the clocks out of the bathroom window.

They worry what might happen if they made him angry. They don't want to know what he might try and break. The building remembers when the ghost of the boy was alive. The building liked it more back then, when children broke.

These ones are too young for the building and so he lets them be.

Flat 101

He can hear the party through the wall. The walls are too thin here. In the mornings, he can hear her shower and he presses his ear against the wall. She sings Billie Holiday sometimes, and those are his favourite days. His view from the only window in his flat is out on to the alleyway that runs alongside the building. It's where the bins are and so, sometimes, when they are overflowing, foxes come and tear them open. He doesn't mind the smell so much. He enjoys watching them play in the litter. The litter in the litter, he says to himself. The building likes that. Sometimes the man forgets things; his mind just goes completely blank (   ) and he snaps back and doesn't remember it. There are spaces within him.

He might be the one. The building is almost sure of it.

The Corridor, First Floor

It is the space that was once an office. The building remembers where the desk was, where the papers were filed. It was a mill, once upon a time; spinning cotton and stinking of oil and sweat, floorboards creaking beneath the weary feet of workers. The smoke billowing across the floor, never escaping, collecting at windows, tapping on them. Let me out. The shadows of the afternoon creeping underneath machines like children. There were children then too, as there are children now, but they did not last long. There was disease, and accidents. Things were lost. It remembers the window that looked out on to the rest of the mill. Remembers a man standing there, watching. How he hated them all. Why had he been so angry? It was a contagious anger; a thing that seeped through the man and dripped from him, and found cracks in the floorboards and the wall. Soaked itself into the building, until the building became hateful too; wires began to fray and disconnect, machines worked so infrequently that it became a running joke, until it became dangerous. The walls felt so much higher and darker then, as though they were closing in, forcing themselves upon the workers. The building at that time masked people's senses, frustrated them, cooked them in the heat from the mill floor. It found (   ) there too, and it liked them. All of this, it powered the building and that power spilled from it, and it became the centre of something. And things were built around it, and they didn't know it, but the people worshipped it. Became its brethren.

How hard would it be to do that again?

How difficult to devolve these people?

Flat 102

The party is quieting down now. There are just a handful of people left, and they have retreated to the sofas and comfy chairs. Wine is still poured, but talk now is softer, more relaxed.

'Must be nice,' the instigator of all conversations says, 'to not have to work all day.'

'I do work,' Mike replies. 'It's maybe not quite the same as you, but I do work.'

'No, no, mate. I'm not trying to have a go or anything. It's fine. You can tell us, we're all friends here. I mean, come on, you what, own a few properties and fleece students on rent, not much more to do now is there?'

'There's a bit more to it than that.'

Other people are now visibly uncomfortable. At least one person leaves the room and heads to the kitchen to pretend to pour themselves another drink.

'I'm sure there is.'

Mike stands, leaves a half full glass of beer on the table next to him. 'Cath, where did you put the coats? I'm going to head if you don't mind.'

'I'm just messing with you. It's fine. I didn't mean anything by it.'

Flat 322

They have stopped playing with the boy. The children are in bed now, pretending to be asleep, their eyes tight shut. The building watches the boy, who stands between the two beds, wondering if they really are just pretending.

He will find out soon.

Flat 101

More and more the building is sure of him. The lights are off in the flat, and the television is on, dancing strobe across the room. He is

watching (   ) but it's going in one ear, out the other. He has
a blanket over his legs. His room is colder than everyone else's in the
building. Heat rises and he is at the bottom. He doesn't switch his
heating on. Not even during the winter. How could he when all the
other people would benefit. He's not paying their bills. Not a chance.
He thinks about his daughter, about phoning her. Even picks up the
handset before changing his mind. She can call him. Why hasn't she?
Why hasn't she been bothered to pick up her own phone and dial
his number? It's not even a case of dialling anymore is it? Not now
everyone's got mobiles. She just has to find his name on a list and
touch it. How difficult is that? Much, much harder for him. He has to
remember the number, or find it in his book. Handwriting's terrible
anyway so he probably wouldn't even be able to read it. Eyes aren't
what they used to be neither.

This is how the building has to do it now. Seep in through the
cracks and darkness. Infect. Find the broken people, the ones who
have gaps, and fill those gaps. Become a small part of them. Take it
from there.

The building finds a gap. (   ) There are plenty here to
choose from.

Flat 322
The boy looks from one bed to the other. Eeney meeney…

Flat 102
His coat is under all of the rest. Mike looks at the pile as though
they've done this on purpose. Just something that they knew would
piss him off. He tears through the pile and throws the other coats and
bags on the floor. Leaves them there. Fuck you.

He doesn't turn the light off.

Leaves the door wide open in case the dog decides it wants to piss
all over their silk bedsheets.

Piss probably doesn't come off silk. Does it?

Flat 322
…miney moe.

The Corridor, First Floor

The building teases out the gaps. Finds them in the party, where animosity already grows. It sees the shape of a boy, filling out the gap between two children, the way that billows of smoke did all those years ago. How it misses the smoke and the fumes. It misses industry and oil, machinery and labour. It can still feed now, it would never have stood this long if it hadn't been able to, but it is so hard. These people are not tired and angry, not in the same way. They do not feed their hate into the building willingly.

It has to take.

Flat 102

He considers not saying goodbye to anyone but it's not quite easy enough. The guests are all sitting in the living room, which blocks the door. The building can feel him now. The building is in his head. Mike wants some sort of commotion after he's gone. He imagines people searching for him. What could have possibly happened to him? But that fantasy is unlikely.

He steps into the room, coat on.

'I'm off now.'

Someone holds their hand up to say goodbye. The rest don't seem to have heard him.

Should he repeat himself? Could sound really stupid if he does. Like he wants the attention.

Flat 322

The building so rarely notices the finer details of people. It knows the boy. The boy only has one hand. The children haven't noticed this. The building does not know if the children understand that the boy is not alive. Do they see how he drifts in and out of their lives? How, when he opens his mouth to speak, no sound comes out?

They will.

Flat 101

He is up and out of his chair. The blanket lies on the floor, trailing along the cold wooden boards. There is a bowl of crisps. Crumbs scattered across the table. He can hear them now in the flat next door. Muffled goodbyes. Someone is leaving.

He feels the (building fills the gap and helps him understand what to do) and he heads to the kitchen. There is (just ignore me it's okay it's okay it's okay this is what you are supposed to do) and so he doesn't question it any further.

Flat 102

They finally look up at him. He's been standing there for a few minutes, coat on. The way they look at him, he cannot tell whether they are surprised that he is leaving, or shocked to find him still there, standing like an idiot in the hallway. He holds his hand up, considers saying goodbye again, doesn't, and steps forwards towards the door. The instigator places his bottle of beer on the table next to him, stands and walks towards Mike.

'You going?'

'Going.' That's all he manages before above them

Flat 322

The boy wakes the children. He couldn't pick just one, no matter where the rhyme landed. He couldn't. He just wants to play. Always just wants to play. They wouldn't wake up at first. He tried to pull the blankets, but they wriggled and turned and fell back asleep. He tried to whisper in their ears but, as always, they couldn't hear him, couldn't quite understand him. In the end, he picked up a handful of their toys – little trucks and cars, some dolls, a large book about space – and threw them straight at the pillows.

The children wake,

Flat 102

screaming. From the flat upstairs?

'Poor kids,' one of them says, 'Nightmares I suppose.'

'I used to get the night terrors too when I was their age. Might even still have a book somewhere on the shelf. American written, but it's still good. My parents used the techniques to help me, and according to them, two weeks into the programme, I was good as gold. Sleep like a baby now.' She looks around, no-one has gotten the joke so she laughs out loud herself. 'Like a baby!' Mike watches her from the doorway. The instigator has opened it.

The corridor outside looks cold.

'Well then,' the instigator says, 'pleasure as always. Drive safe.'

Never have five words been said with less accuracy.

Mike nods and leaves. As the door closes, the last thing he hears is that

Flat 322

they don't want to play, but the boy knows something is coming. There is a rumbling and he can feel it. It shakes the pipes and rattles the bed frames. In the kitchen right now the plates are shaking and shattering in the cupboards, he promises. He just wants one last game before it all changes. Just one last game. Hopscotch? Tic Tac Toe? That new one that the children taught him: British Bulldog. He imagines running from one side of the room to the other. He imagines the children trying to catch him. Oh how he'd run and run. Press his hands against the wall. Hand.

The building sees him. He sees the building.

The building is nearly done.

The Corridor, First Floor

one of the women is saying, 'I used to piss the bed until I was seven, but then we all had our problems growing up, didn't we?'

Then the door closes and it's just him in the corridor. The lights – on a timer – flicker on and he makes his way down towards the door. Above, he can hear the stamping of feet. The children from upstairs, he assumes. There is a crashing and he laughs to himself.

This is the kind of stupid place where it would happen, isn't it? He'd just turn around and there she'd be. Dot Cotton, brandishing a knife. Would she say anything? Why would she do it? In the soap opera he's created in his head he imagines that he slighted her in some awful way. Insulted her in the pub. Cheated on her in some pre-watershed bedroom antics. The fans would hate him, of course. They couldn't wait for him to leave the show. When the newspapers revealed that he was going to be killed off – oh how they would celebrate.

And this, he thinks, is exactly how it would be done.

The lights flicker again. They dim. They go off.

A door, just next to the flat he left, unlocks and swings open.

The lights flicker on.

(Then off)

|A Moment Could Last Them Forever|

∿

She has inherited her father's gift, in her own way.

The streetlamp buzzes outside, and the rattle of a bus tinkles the spoon on the saucer. She grips hold of her tea. Her client totters in with a plate of cakes, store bought, and smiles a wrinkle-creased smile.

'Here.' She offers the plate. 'Guests have the first pick.'

Her name is Edna, she lives alone and got in touch through the church group. There are always whispers from the church group, a drifting of recommendation. Often they just want to speak to a loved one: husband, brother, father; sometimes it's a celebrity and sometimes, when she's really lucky, they want to know their futures. Not that any of them have much of one. Her circuit, if it can be called as much, is the living rooms, kitchens and conservatories of the retired, ill and lonely. She doesn't talk to the dead, not in the way her father did, although she privately jokes to herself that her clients tend to be close enough.

She takes the plate from Edna and picks a cake as though selecting a weapon in a dual to the death.

'I want to speak to my Victor,' Edna says. 'I want to know if he's happy, and if he hears me when I speak to him.' She picks up her tea, hands shaking, and touches the rim of the mug to her lips, tilting it slightly, carefully. She looks pale, her skin thinning, losing colour. 'Can you help me?'

'I do things different, did they tell you that?'

'Yes, they said something like that.'

'I don't do Ouija boards or séances or anything. Now, do you have it?'

Edna nods, and stands again, 'It's in the kitchen, I did like you said on the phone; seven days?'

'Yes, that should do it.'

Edna leaves the room again. The older crowd, her only crowd really, tend not to produce the best results. She remembers doing this at University: lines scrawled across enormous maps of the city, strange sigils along roads, by-ways, motorways, and riversides. The most recent in still-wet ink, and the oldest a fading black, the ink drying and dying. She shudders, thinking about those years, doing readings at house parties, being the weird girl. Edna comes back in, and it is immediately clear that this isn't going to be the wildest of readings. She has a small fold out road map of Hither Green. The road they are on, scribbled on several times with a black pen, scratching a deep groove into the page. The line leads from the house, up the road to the high street, the supermarket, and the church.

'As you can tell, I don't get out much,' Edna explains. She hasn't yet taken a piece of cake for herself.

'That's fine, don't worry. It'll still work. The most important thing is that we don't lie; it doesn't work if we lie. As long as this is a real week for you, and represents everywhere you went, we can work with it.' There is no answer, so she assumes Edna is telling the truth. She takes a blank piece of paper from her bag, and several marker pens, and then removes the light box: a part from an old projector she found in the dump.

'Have you got a socket?'

She places the map on the light box and switches it on. It buzzes louder than the streetlamp outside, and she can feel the heat coming off it already. She unfolds the map as far as she can and places it on top of the box; the light barely shines through, but the lines are clearly lit up. She places the blank, opaque sheet of paper over the top of the map, and the lines bleed through from underneath like shadows. She pauses for a moment, her hand wavering over the selection of marker pens, and she picks a medium thick one first, tracing the line from Edna's home, down the road to the high street. A daily trip by the looks of it, an arterial vessel, with little capillary veins running out to the other places, trailing away. She takes a thinner pen for those. Edna doesn't say much whilst she recreates the map. Sometimes they comment on their activities. *That's when my son took me out for dinner.* Or, *I go dancing every Thursday: ballroom.* She feels sorry for Edna, and wonders whether she even wants any of this, whether all she wants is some company.

'Have you got a bowl? Something you don't mind getting burned?'

'Burned? What are you going to do? I don't want my net curtains catching.'

'It won't spread. I've done this plenty of times before.' She switches the light box off and holds up the piece of paper, the lines now out of context, an inverted L with tiny spidery tendrils running off. 'It's a kind of sigil,' she explains, 'Think of it like static, do you know about static electricity? Like a Van De Graff. You run it and it builds up and builds up until you release the energy. It's a bit like that. You can build up and build up all these thoughts about yourself, or anyone over the week, and this shape here,' she holds the piece of paper up so Edna can see, 'is a symbol of all that built up energy. All we have to do is release it.'

'And the fire will do that?'

'Oh yes, burning works spectacularly.'

Edna brings a bowl from the kitchen and places it in the middle of the table. She holds on to it for just a moment, as though considering whether she really wants to ruin the bowl, and eventually lets go.

'Here.' She passes Edna the piece of paper. 'Put that in the bowl, and then we set fire to it. It was your husband wasn't it? That's who you wanted to contact?' Edna nods. 'OK then, just keep him in your mind. Is there something you remember strongly about him? Something significant?'

'He wore Old Spice.'

'Just keep thinking about that.' Edna shuts her eyes tight. 'No, no, you can keep your eyes open. I need you to place the paper in the bowl; if you keep your eyes shut, you might miss it.' She snaps them open again and picks up the piece of paper, lowering it into the bowl.

'Here,' she hands the lighter to Edna. 'It's best if you light it.'

After, she smokes outside in Edna's garden. The grass is a little overgrown, and when she walks through it, pacing as she always does, she can feel the wetness of dew from the unmowed grass seep into her tights, ankle high. She turns to look at the house, the dim light from the living room flickers. The rumble of traffic is lessening as the night bears down. She can see Edna in the house, sat in the chair, crying silently, but she is just a faded kind of shadow. There are no stars out, just a thick cloud. She's heard that there's a gale coming, although the night is still. Edna opens the back door. 'Do you want another cup of tea?' She doesn't appear to be shaken. She has promised Edna that she'll do it again, at no extra cost, in a week or so. She doesn't think that it will do any good. It's the journey. There is a rustling in the bushes, probably a fox or a cat, and she stubs her cigarette out, heads back inside the house, and leaves immediately.

A week has not added much to Edna's journeying.

'I tried to head out a bit more,' she said, passing over the map. 'Of course, I had to go to the bookstore to buy a new road map, but because I didn't have it with me, I didn't mark it up, should I have done? Will this not work again?'

'I shouldn't think that would matter.' She thinks it might, but she won't say anything.

Edna has coated the room in Old Spice, his last bottle apparently. 'You said it would help,' she explains. 'I've been listening to his old records. Couldn't bring myself to wear his clothes though. Got out one of his old jumpers and put my arm through the sleeve, but it felt like it was too far.'

They repeat the procedure and again, the results are timid at best. Last week she was sure she heard a low moan coming from inside the bowl, a coming of *something*, and this week: not even that. There may, she concedes afterwards with Edna, have been a flash of purple light, but that may have just been one of the limos ferrying twenty-something girls to a hen party somewhere in the city.

'I don't want you to get your hopes up,' she says to Edna, 'this isn't an exact science.'

She leaves Edna's, promising to return next week, knowing it will still not work. 'Maybe,' she says, 'you should get out some photos of him. Try to think back to the times you spent with him. Maybe that will help build up a good atmosphere.'

'Do you think he might not be here? That maybe he's just gone for good? Am I not good enough to haunt?' Edna has plenty of questions.

'I'm sure he's here,' she says, and to reinforce it she places her hand on Edna's arm. She wonders if it all seems too forced. She remembers something her father said, 'To know that they're not alone for a moment, that could last them forever.' Edna shuts the door, leaving her standing in the unlit porch. She trudges back to the bus stop, her bag weighing her down.

She has other clients. There is the milkman who is sure his mother occupies the welsh-dresser, rattling the thin, delicate china and drinking the gin. There is the young just-married couple, frightened to sleep at night for the thing that lies in bed, keeping them apart. Then there is the middle-aged woman, who cries on her shoulder about her young son, as they burn her little tube map in a mixing bowl. They, all of them, work. There are results and endings. When she leaves, they tell her that she has changed their lives, that they will be happier. She can't help but think of Edna.

Later in the week, Edna phones her in the middle of the night. She answers the phone half asleep, waking from a dream about a meal she has been eating inside her father's stomach.

'I think I heard him,' Edna wails from the other end.

'You didn't hear him.'

'He said, *I miss you Eddie, I miss you*, and then he smashed the glass that had my false teeth in.'

'I don't think he said that.'

'I think now might be the perfect time, can you come to the house now? I've got the map handy.'

She looks at her bedside clock. The streetlamp outside her window has broken again, so the clock is the only source of light in the room.

'It's half four in the morning.'

'I really think this is what was missing. I can pay you double. I just want to speak to him one more time.'

'Good night.'

She lies still in her bed, staring up at the ceiling where the paper peels away from a damp patch, eager to escape. She wonders if maybe she could pretend to get in touch with Edna's husband, just a little flight of fancy. Rig a wire to knock a cup over, or plant a tape recorder with some garbled Hallmark message in. Just thinking about it makes her shudder. She had seen the frauds at play in darkened theatres, with earpieces and assistants. At least she had the courage to admit when it wasn't working, although there hasn't been anyone she's failed. Not yet. But why is it so difficult for her to get through with Edna?

She tries to sleep, and, as always, dreams of herself stretched thin like wires across the roads near her father's house.

Edna has prepared everything this week.

She arrives promptly, and Edna has already made her a cup of tea. They sit down in the living room. She notices the floor is strewn with photos of Edna's husband: wedding pictures, holiday snaps, and several particularly revealing private shots. Edna is wearing a jumper which clearly belonged to him. She smells of Old Spice (*I bought some more, just for this*). She even looks different. Her face, which had been thin and pale but happy, looks more tired, more sad. It's the same withered, Victorian expression her husband has in the photographs. Edna hands her a bowl of stew.

'It was his favourite,' she explains. 'He always cooked it. I thought it might help.'

It smells rich and warm. Edna hands her a map, this one bigger and more expansive, with side streets and alleys marked out clearly. Her journeys have become wider, far reaching. There are regular trips into the city, lines criss-crossing and intertwining, meandering around the roads like forgotten string. There is no symbol, there is no pattern. This is confusion and fear. This is looking to escape, to run away and hide. This is desperation.

Once, she recorded her own journeys across the city, marking them down on a scrawny map, spindly lines tracing her journey to work and back again. When she looked at it properly at the end of the week she saw a perfectly shaped V. An arrow pointing her away from the city, away from everything. It was then that she got too scared to burn it, too scared to see whatever wanted her to leave, whatever brushed past her hair at night, tilted the paintings on her wall and switched the TV channels over at whim.

She looks at Edna and understands that fear is not always about what is there, lurking in the shadows, but that what is there might not be what you were looking for. That what you were looking for was never there.

That they are gone.

Edna plays her husband's favourite record. The Kinks' 'Village Green Preservation Society'. The needle jumps at first, but then settles in as the music spatters out of the old speakers in the corner. She has the same bowl from the other weeks; the charcoaled remains of the previous attempts still lie in the basin. Edna closes the curtains, and dims the lights.

Her eyes adjust to the lack of light, and she watches Edna take her seat. She flicks the light box on, placing another blank sheet over it, and then begins to outline the shape Edna has created. She finds that, instead of just tracing over it, making it just another shape, it is easier to start at the house on the map, and take the journeys with her. She follows the road down the hill to the train station, and imagines the tip of her pen is waiting at the platform, watching the train pull in slowly, and then sitting in the carriage watching as the blanket terrace houses pass her by as she heads into the city. She follows the line around the streets, into shops and down alleys, she doubles back on herself several times, stopping off in shops and cafes, browsing bookstores, before turning back to the station. The line doesn't head home straight away. Instead, it stops off halfway up, somewhere around London Bridge, and continues along, down the river. This is a filter of a filter of a life. The resulting scribble on the page is not like the previous weeks, it seems muddled and random: there is no symbol, nothing that seems to hold any meaning. She looks up at Edna, who is wringing her hands to stop them from shaking.

She passes her the sheet of paper and Edna places it in the bowl, and then lights it.

When she lights her cigarette outside, the wind has died down and there is a calm in the garden. A solitary cardigan hangs from a washing line in front of her, and somewhere nearby, next door perhaps, there is the hollow sound of someone moving a wheelie-bin. She feels relief for the first time in weeks. Edna is sat in her chair in the living room. The pictures have settled and the bowl has crashed spectacularly to the floor, the ash rising from the splinters and forming rudimentary words and pictures in the air, before disintegrating. There was a voice, and although all she heard was a vague murmur, Edna swears it was her dear husband. More power to her.

As she sits smoking, a small fox treads through the grass, finding its way into the garden through a gap in the wall next to her. It's young, and its thin, lithe body slinks across the garden. It stops halfway across and stares at her. Under the moon, the fox casts strange shadows so that its body appears twisted, and its arms and legs are stretched and elongated. She watches it. The two of them keep their eyes on one another for what seems like forever. Then, it turns and walks away, and she holds her finger up and traces its path across the garden, memorising the shape and immortalising it.

|Beneath the Pavement, the Beach|

~

The First City

The singer leant back, away from the mic, and yelled, 'Fuck Punk, it's dead now.' He chucked the empty bottle into the crowd. 'To Saint Joe Strummer!' he said, counting in the rest of the band. She stood at the front and danced with tears in her eyes that night, in love with the music, with the crowd at The Roadhouse, and mourning her hero. When she'd seen the news she knew she had to get out of her bedsit and find some music, any music, just to get the thoughts from her head. Someone in the band, the bassist maybe, handed her a can of Red Stripe and she chugged it. There were barely fifty people in the dingy venue, though it felt cramped and full, thanks to the low ceiling which brushed against her head whenever she jumped up. She made eyes with the bassist and he smiled at her.

She hung out after the gig, waiting by the green room door, staring at the scrawled signatures of bands who'd played there before they got big. There were names there she recognised, and she felt a pang of guilt, wishing she'd seen them here, wishing she'd got in there before they wound up on the Pyramid stage or wherever she'd first seen them.

He came out carrying his guitar and gave her that same smile again. He was glad to see her.

'I was hoping you'd still be here.'

'Well,' she said, 'I owe you a pint, don't I?'

They went with the rest of the band up the road to Dry Bar, and without her knowing a drink landed in front of her, so she shouted a thank you to no one in particular. The singer was already drunk, and when she thought about it she remembered a greasy swagger that he'd had on stage. He was older than the rest, with greying, wiry hair, and a grin that showed off the creases in his face. The rest of the band, and the others who'd come along to the bar with them, all sat in a booth on sofas. She perched at the edge with the bassist and listened to the singer holding court.

'Moved here in the eighties because of them, that Free Trade Hall gig man, that was it. You know everyone who went there formed a band. That's what I thought this city was, so I came here, but look at it.' He gestured out of the window, and she saw the rain cascading down. Funny, she realised that she barely noticed it. 'Fucking grey and wet and all the musicians here want to be New fucking Order. Strummer man, he was the shit and now it's all over.' He raised his pint, 'to the Women Underneath,' and the rest of the band followed. She found herself doing the same thing, though she didn't know really what they meant. The bassist put his arm around her and she allowed it.

'Ignore him,' the bassist said, 'he gets like this every night. You watch, he'll get worse and he'll fire the lot of us, then tomorrow he'll wake up and book another rehearsal space, like it never even happened.'

She looked around the rest of the bar. It was busy, full of students and tourists. The DJ, tucked away in a booth embedded in the wall, segued from 'Atmosphere' to 'God's Cop'.

'This, this is what I'm talking about,' the singer yelled. 'Fucking Anderton. You know when he became Chief Constable for the city he told everyone he had a direct line to God? He hated the city, turned it into hell for anyone who wanted to enjoy it. Drinkers, dancers, hell, if you were gay, he especially hated you. He wasn't talking to God. Never. God's dead. The Women Underneath devoured him.'

Later, she stood outside under the canopy to catch some fresh air and the bassist came back with another drink. They drank together silently for a while, watching the buses pass, the yellow lights within them looking warm and inviting.

'Thanks for tonight,' she said.

'Hell of a gig. Are you heading home tonight?' He put his arm around her.

She turned and kissed him.

'Tear enough of this city down and you can reach the core of the earth,' the singer mumbled, slamming the door of the bar open. He looked at the bassist. 'Traitor.'

The singer stumbled and fell, taking a chair and table with him as he did. They helped him up and the bassist said, 'Look, he just lives a few roads over, ten-minute walk tops. Help me get him back?'

'Sure.'

They crossed through the Northern Quarter and out past the Arndale, the singer held up by the two of them. Just behind Victoria station, whilst they stopped to let him vomit, the bassist pointed to a block of flats.

'He lives up there, not far now. Sorry about this. I ruined the night didn't I?'

'This is an adventure, you've ruined nothing.'

The bassist dug a set of keys out of the singer's pocket and let them into the building. The lights flickered on, sensing their motion, and the three of them piled into the tiny lift. The bassist pressed the button for the fourth floor. The block would have been modern and fancy if she'd visited it a few years ago. Now, several bulbs were broken, flickering and strobing; someone had taken a key to the floor numbers written on the side of the elevator, scratching them off, making them barely readable. *Another forgotten place on the edge of the city*, she thought.

The lift rumbled up without an announcement. She felt as though they were being watched, and she looked across to the singer, trying to see if he was awake. His eyes remained closed and she looked around, feeling the building itself was watching her, judging her. The lift rumbled on and she felt a strange sensation, as though the lift was moving slowly down rather than up.

'Did we press the right floor?' she asked, but the bassist said nothing.

When the lift stopped and the doors opened, she could see a black expanse in front of her. The air was cool and somewhere in the distance, echoing around them, water dripped. *It's a cavern*, she wanted to say, but it was a fleeting thought.

'How far along does he live?'

'Just a bit further.'

The two of them struggled along with the singer, each of them with an arm around their shoulders. She could barely see anything in front of them and they didn't pass any doorways.

Then the air changed, warming up, and she struggled with her breath. There was moisture hanging around them. In her arms, the singer stirred.

'Is he okay?'

She turned to look at the bassist but the darkness had enveloped them all. Behind her, she heard the distant ping of the lift, then the rise of it.

'I thought he lived on the fourth floor. We're in the basement, aren't we?'

The weight on her shoulder vanished, and she realised she was alone.

'Hey, guys? Hey?' Her voice came back to her, as if replying to the question. *Hey.*

She reached out and felt a breeze. The singer and the bassist, if they were both here, were no longer next to her.

Up ahead, a sliver of light flashed. Instruments were being tuned and the myriad sounds of a crowd could be heard as though on the other side of a wall.

She approached the sliver of light, and pushed against it.

The Second City

She took a tram into the city. It was the solstice, and it felt as though Manchester hadn't seen the sun at all that day. The Met line had changed and she couldn't pinpoint when that had happened. All of a sudden, it seemed, the tramcars had become yellow, and the seats had been all but torn out. When she looked at the route map, lines stretched across the city to places she had never heard of before: Hollinwood, Freehold, and Shadowmoss. They existed before, she is sure of it, but they feel more present and real now. This city is full of places unknown to her and she wondered if the people who lived in Shadowmoss felt the same way about Southern Cemetery, Stretford, or Navigation Road, the places she lived her whole life.

The tram curved around the Hilton and G-Mex and into the city. She got off at Piccadilly Gardens and walked to The Roadhouse from there. Atherton's lot were out in force, but she knew which streets they didn't bother with. God's Cop patrolled Canal Street and the adjoining waterways. They claimed they were fishing revellers out of the water, but that wasn't true. She'd heard from friends that they beat gay lads up on the boats. Dragged them from the cobbled pathways onto the decks and fucked them up.

She chucked a couple of quid at the guy at the ticket counter and he stamped her hand, even though she was underage. Some shitty metal band were being played through the speakers whilst the guys she'd come to see were sound checking, no doubt whatever she could hear was the product of the lanky skinhead behind the bar, black bar tats all up his arms, covering up whatever stupid political slogans he'd gotten years ago that he no longer agreed with.

The band onstage were called The Stains. She'd heard a song of theirs on a Kerrang CD a month or so previously and loved them. They were loud, and angry, but their influences stretched beyond music. In an interview in the magazine, they'd said all the right words like CL Nolan, Hookland, and Ballard. Like her, they hated the city but they loved it too. How could you not?

The band looked familiar to her, but she dismissed the thought. So many bands, all looking the same. Grown-up kids in their late twenties who listened to too much of The Strokes. She grabbed a pint and made her way to the front. Not hard to do in a crowd of thirty.

There were faces she recognised amongst the people in the room. No one she could name, but people she'd danced with, drunk with, sung along with. She always came to these places alone. A part of her felt she didn't belong here, even though she was born here, had lived here her entire life. It was as though there was another city she had known and that was Manchester. This place here, it didn't feel real.

After the music had stopped and the singer had asked her backstage, they lay together on the settee in the green room and she stared at the signatures scrawled and etched into the walls.

'You know,' he said, slurring his words and not really looking at her. 'When I was a kid, we lived in these tiny council flats in Oldham. The walls were so thin you could hear everything going on all around you. There was this flat below us, it was empty, no one had lived there in years and the council never housed anyone there, but every night I could hear this woman, just walking around crying. One night I got out of the flat and I posted some food through the letterbox. I thought she was hungry, that's all. The cries stopped then.

'Sometimes when I look at the city I think it's like her. The woman underneath. It just wants to be fed. People have tried all sorts, they've fed it music and books and art, and sometimes they've bled for it. Every time we give something to it, it absorbs it, the good and the bad.'

She was drunk and she felt like she'd lost control, and so she made her excuses and left.

Walking down the canal she saw two policemen fishing a boy out of the river with a long pole. They were smirking. The boy was bloated, dead; that much she could tell when she passed him by. His face was blue and red, veins popped and bleeding within him. How long had he been in the water? The two officers watched her as she passed by them and she picked up her pace, hurrying along. Up ahead, the gaping mouth of a tunnel stood. On the other side was Castlefield, the edge of the city, and beyond, Salford. The other city. Behind her, one of the officers said something, a question directed at her. She ignored it and quickened. There was a panic in her now, and she thought about what the singer had said, and as she entered into the tunnel she thought about how she would never leave the city, that she had fed herself to it a long time ago and was only now disappearing into its mouth.

The Eighth City

The buildings were listening, watching. There were only flats in Ancoats, old warehouses gutted and transformed, but the skin remained. In the basement, amongst the parked cars, she found an old piece of machinery, thick black paint coating cogs and levers. Inside, it was the only reminder of what this place used to be. When the pipes groaned and the walls creaked and expanded, it was the ghost of what used to be there talking to them, threatening them. A man two floors down had killed himself three weeks earlier. He had broken the locks on the windows and thrown himself down into the Rochdale Canal below. Just one of so many who had drowned in that stretch of water, amongst discarded shopping trolleys and used condoms.

The band were on at nine, and she got to Big Hands early, finding a settee near to where the band were setting up. The red glow from the lights made the place feel seedy, though it was anything but. She was in student territory, and did her best to mark herself out from them.

She'd been nursing a pint for an hour before someone stopped in front of her and said, 'Do I know you?' Staring deep into her eyes. He sat down before she had a chance to reply and say *no*.

'Maybe I don't,' he continued, 'but you look so familiar.'

He sat and talked with her whilst the rest of the band set up. Fallowfield was where his flat was, where the buildings were malicious and slippery. Just last week, a row of terrace houses swallowed their residents up whole. On the border, near Rusholme and the curry mile, people lived in a makeshift shanty town. He'd befriended his room. That's how he described it. She had never heard of anyone doing that before. Didn't know it was even possible.

'It's all just harmonics really,' he explained between swigs. 'I can show you, if you like?'

It's a line. Of course it is. But she can't help but be intrigued.

They caught the Magic Bus up the road. Condensation, the sweat of people pouring out of clubs and bars, steamed the windows, and she drew pictures. Somewhere, just before the curry mile, the top deck started singing 'Wonderwall' and she couldn't help but join in, even though she hated the thing. The bus wouldn't be listening. That was a right reserved for the bricks and mortar of the city, ancient Victorian workhouses, warehouses, terraces. They chose who got to stay.

He sat in the seat next to her, arm stretched behind, holding on to the headrest. She kept her hands on her lap. Not touching him. Not giving any kind of a hint. She was curious, but the men in the city had a darkness within them. Something behind their eyes. The way the buildings did, how the walls felt like eyes, and the groaning pipes hissed whispered threats.

They got off and walked to his flat, he'd had his arm around her the whole time. She hadn't noticed, or cared.

'You know,' he said, 'I might write a song about you.'

'Please don't.'
He kissed her instead.

The buildings hushed them to sleep, so calm and peaceful. *Come now,* they whispered, *let us take care of you.* She had learned long ago not to listen to the walls, but here, in his place, she felt a curious comfort. It was hours later when she woke. She climbed out of his bed and walked down the corridor to find the loo. The bathroom ceiling was mouldy, black spots blossoming out from the corners of the room, spreading across, tendrils reaching out. Outside, the rain was heavy, battering against the window. Nature telling her to wake up; to leave.

She sometimes wondered why it was that the buildings were like this, in this city. The phenomenon had not been discovered in Liverpool or Leeds, or Nottingham, not even London, where the ghosts of history clawed at the concrete, desperate to come up for air. This building had been a factory, long ago. Children creeping beneath machinery, losing limbs, the air taking years off their lives. Now, only the exposed brickwork, timber trusses and its name, nostalgically reeling people in. The Mills.

She flicked the bathroom light off and headed back to the hallway, but it was darker than she remembered. She tried to feel for the door but it was no longer there. Somewhere distant, she heard whispered voices and she thought for a moment that it was the building itself. Was this how it happened, how they lured people close? How all of those whom the buildings vanished slipped from this world? But that didn't feel right. The voice wasn't malevolent. She could barely hear it, but she recognised the tone of it. *Come to us. There is another world.*

How could she have known they were saying that?

She walked down the hallway and, finally, gave herself up to the dark.

The Nineteenth City

Mad one she was having. No sooner were they through the doors at 42nd Street when one of the bouncers chucked a couple of test tube shots at her and said, 'On the house, love.'

Sometime late in the night, harmonising to whatever-the-fuck-it-was with a stranger in the toilets, the news broke and the DJ stopped the music.

'Noel Gallagher's died,' they said over the PA.

Car accident out in Morocco or some shit was what they were saying. The DJ immediately played 'Wonderwall' and everyone sang along until she couldn't hear the words.

Two of the bar staff were comforting each other in a hug, so she nabbed a couple of cans of Red Stripe and tried to lose herself in the crowd. The mood had changed. Kids in baggy pants weeping on the dance floor. She pushed through them all and left the place.

Somewhere out past John Rylands, she had the urge to leave Manchester, a drunken decision that she would go and never come back. Stupid idea.

She turned down Bridge Street and headed for Salford. The other city.

The bridge over the Irwell separated the two cities. *If I can get there,* she thought, *it will be okay.* Five cans, two shots and whatever the fuck else she'd had, and suddenly walking across a bridge felt like the biggest damned decision she'd ever made. As though doing this would make all the bad stuff just go away, Not Gallagher, who gave a shit, right? But the other things. The things that had made this city feel so wrong for the last few years. The jobs and boyfriends and houses. Somewhere along the way she had fed herself to Manchester and it had shat her out in the canals near Ancoats. That's what the city did best.

There was someone in the river. A man, not much older than her. He was face up, but dead. His skin bulging out, lumpy and blue. Another drowned man. Most likely he'd been under for a while, only surfacing now his body had taken on enough water. She got her phone out to call the police and report it, but then she noticed how purposefully he floated up the river, against the current. How straight his body was. Magnetised almost. He was a scally too, tracksuit bottoms tucked into his socks. There'd be a mosher-witch somewhere near Winter Hill waiting for him, spinning hexes with chains and nu-metal patches, so she'd let him be. Let him be food.

Past the Mark Addy she saw the entrance to Salford Central and climbed the steps. A couple of kids passed her by, and her first thought was that they were far too young to be out alone. One of them said, 'Can't believe he's dead.'

'Guess that means Blur won,' said the other, and they carried on.

Up at the top of the steps she looked back at Manchester and she knew the city had changed. The grey clouds of the city used to make it stand out, used to make it feel fucking iconic. But now everything was dulled. Nothing to do with Noel. Nothing at all. The city had been dying for a long time. Maybe since the witches left, opening up their bead shops and tarot parlours in Levy and Rusholme rather than stand to be in the city centre. Maybe it was as far back as the beginning of the city as she knew it, when everyone put dickheads on a pedestal just because they could write a song, made them gods and then got all surprised when they forgot they weren't immortal.

A train was coming.

She could go back. Back into the city, into the club, into the mourning. But the train was coming, and she had to get on it.

Maybe, she thought, the next stop would be Manchester, only this time it would be another Manchester.

As the train pulled in she saw someone else sitting in the carriage. A man from another life.

She opened the door and felt the rain on her face. Looking up she saw skyscraper stalactites hanging down, the water of the city dripping on her. She tasted it, and it tasted of a thousand Manchesters, none of which had a fucking beach. She was underneath it all now, the moonlight of the Hilton bearing down, the Irwell flowing above her. Somewhere distant, she heard footsteps and saw them, all the people walking, and she looked up, waiting for them to catch her eye so she could drag them down with her to the city below.

|Acknowledgements|

The stories in *Hunting by the River* have been a part of my life for so many years, crossing cities and entire lifetimes. I am hugely grateful to Steve J Shaw for picking this up, polishing the sentences and publishing the collection. Thanks also to Dan Coxon, George Sandison, Verity Holloway and Aliya Whiteley who read half of these stories and helped me find what I was trying to do with them. A very big thank you to Ian Carrington, Ben Judge, Abi Hynes, Tom Mason, David Hartley, Beth Underdown and Rob Cutforth who not only gave tons of valuable feedback on these stories, but helped to build such an incredible community of writers in Manchester, where I first started piecing this collection together. The biggest thanks to Nici West, my incredible partner, for putting up with me, and for her insight into most of the stories in this collection. You were right about pretty much everything.

Sadie and Robin, these stories are a bit old for you right now. Ask me to tell them to you another day.

|About the Author|

~

Daniel Carpenter grew up in Manchester and now lives in London with his family. This is his first collection.

Find him on Twitter and Instagram @dancarpenter85